THE GHOSTLY GROOM

A JIM MALHAVEN MYSTERY: BOOK 3

HELEN WHISTBERRY

CONTENTS

OTHER WORKS BY HELEN WHISTBERRY

The Jim Malhaven Mysteries Series:

The Weird Sisters

The Avenging Angel

The Ghostly Groom

Take My Hand at Midnight: A Gothic Ghost Tale

Short stories in the following collections:

Creating Cinderella

Autumn Nights: 12 Chilling Tales for Midnight

Of Cottages and Cauldrons

Villainous

Duplicitous

Ravens and Roses

Autumn Nights: 10 Sinister Stories

In Somnio

ACKNOWLEDGMENTS

A very heartfelt thank you to my beta readers:
Jacob Klop, Eileen Curley Hammond,
Elizabeth Belt, Shawna,
and my beloved sister
for their insightful and honest feedback
and advice on the first draft of this novel.

And big appreciation and love
to my friends on Twitter who cheer me on
in my writing and artistic endeavors.

A single kind thought or encouraging word
can change somebody's life.

"What greater thing is there for two human souls, than to feel that they are joined for life—to strengthen each other in all labor, to rest on each other in all sorrow, to minister to each other in all pain, to be one with each other in silent unspeakable memories at the moment of the last parting?"

— *ADAM BEDE*, GEORGE ELIOT

PROLOGUE

I can't say as I expected to spend my wedding day in a jail cell, accused of offing my new wife's first husband. But then again, given all the weird happenings I'd experienced, maybe I shouldn't have been so surprised when my old pal Joey Flanagan pulled out a set of handcuffs and hauled me away from the altar and my bride just after we said, "I do."

For someone who's gotten used to tangling with ghosts from the past, it was still a doozy of a pill to swallow, being charged with killing Lukasz Jankowski when we'd all thought he was long dead and resting at the bottom of the Atlantic Ocean. It was the look on his widow's face that really hit me in the heart though. Victoria Jankowski is the woman I love with all my jaded soul. I'll never forget how her joy turned to horror all in a second as I was dragged off.

Whether she was horrified for me or of me, I couldn't say and didn't have time to ask. Flanagan don't fool around when he's on the job, and he wasn't about to give a break even to his best friend, not on such a charge as Murder in the First. He and a couple of his boys hustled me away plenty quick.

Now I'm cooped up at the precinct house, sat in an eight-by-eight concrete box, with a not-too-fragrant drunk sleeping it off on one side of me and an annoyingly chatty petty thief on the other, with no end in sight. At least it gives me plenty of time to think back on how it all came to this.

CHAPTER ONE

It wasn't so long ago I was groaning and moaning from an aching back as I pulled the last few weeds from a flowerbed around my humble abode. Just like in the song, June was busting out all over Wynter's Hill Cemetery. I'd taken up gardening as a hobby since I'd moved into the caretaker's cottage on the grounds when Victoria relocated to the big house. It kept me out of trouble and helped Victoria out now she was busy learning the ropes of being heir to the Wynter family fortune.

Victoria was gonna make a beautiful June bride. We'd decided to get hitched back in March just before Eastertime, but it had taken a while for Victoria to convince her aunt, one Livinia Cressley née Wynter, to agree to the plot. Liv held the purse strings, and while Victoria would've walked away from the money without a second thought, I didn't want to break up what little family she had left.

Liv's no fan of Jim Malhaven, and in a way, I can't say I blame her. A rough-edged, two-bit reporter with the local paper with a scar across half his face that makes him look like an extra in a gangster B-movie and who rarely has two bills in his pocket to rub together ain't prime marriage material. But Victoria saw something in me, and I was grateful she did. I couldn't imagine being in a world without her ever since we'd first met when I was investigating a haunting at the cemetery she called home the previous fall.

That's right. We'd known each other less than a year and were already planning on getting hitched, but we'd clicked almost from the start once we got a few misunderstandings out of the way. I'd come close to having my head aerated by a bullet twice since then. Leaves you with the notion we don't always got all the time left we think we do, so we decided to get a move on once Victoria persuaded Liv she meant business.

Victoria had been a widow for over six years, ever since her husband had gone down with his Navy ship in November of '44. She'd given birth to a daughter only a few days after getting the visit from the Western Union telegram delivery boy everyone dreaded in those days. Her daughter didn't survive more than a few months herself, leaving Victoria all alone and likely to remain so until yours truly happened along. From all reports, Lukasz had been a good man and I had no intention of replacing him in her heart, just squeezing in there beside the husband and child she'd always mourn.

No one was more surprised than me when Victoria took a shine to such a palooka as myself, except maybe my friend Joey Flanagan. While I turned to reporting after the war, Joey became a cop on the beat until he got promoted to detective. He never tired of pretending amazement I had "landed such a good-looking dish," as he liked to put it, until I threatened to punch him if he didn't stop talking that way about a lady.

He's not wrong though. With her honey-blonde hair and stormy blue eyes, Victoria turns heads wherever she goes, but it's her calm warmth, her open nature that get me. It may sound funny coming from a six-foot-four brute, but I feel safe when I'm around her. Both the war and some unfortunate violence since then that gave me two bum legs and the scar down my face had left me feeling unsettled and unsure of myself. Meeting Victoria was like coming into safe harbor after some hard years adrift and alone.

We'd had some strange adventures together since we met, but somehow, we always got through them. I thought we'd have smooth sailing ahead, but I guess I should've known Jim Malhaven and untroubled waters ain't exactly on speaking terms.

On that particular day, however, I was feeling on top of the world except for my aching back. Things only looked up when Victoria brought me out a cool glass of lemonade from the big house where she lived with her aunt and uncle-in-law.

"Sure hits the spot," I said to her, smacking my lips in satisfaction as we sat side by side on the bench in front of my cottage.

"Seems the least I can do given you won't accept a salary for all your hard work."

"Living rent-free so close to the light of my life and the loveliest lady I know is more than enough payment for me."

"You do say the sweetest things, darling. Will it feel strange moving into the main house once we're married?"

"It has crossed my mind we might be more comfortable here." I waved the fedora I'd pulled down from my head to cool off at the small but cozy caretaker's cottage. "We'd have more privacy anyhow."

"I know, but it would throw Aunt Livinia into a tizzy. Don't worry. Our suite of rooms is all the way on the other side of the house from Livinia and Mr. Cressley—or Cornelius, I should say. Even though he's my uncle by marriage now, I find it hard to get into the habit."

"Yeah, he's kind of a formal guy. Don't seem right to get too familiar with him. I guess I can get used to living up there," I said, looking at the big mansion on the hill that the Wynter family called home, "though it'll be the fanciest joint I ever stayed at. Besides, you probably have a lot of memories from your time in the cottage with Lukasz that you wouldn't want to spoil."

"I don't know. I lived here so much longer without him than with him. It is bittersweet to think back on the short time we had together, but let's look to the future," she said, snuggling close under my outstretched arm. She fit there perfect, and we'd spent many an hour together on that self-same bench in just that position. I wondered if we'd come down and sit there after we got married, or if maybe Victoria was planning on getting a new tenant for the cottage.

She must've read my mind. "I was thinking we'd look for a caretaker after the wedding. Goodness knows we can afford one, and you don't need to be breaking your back out here at your advanced age."

"Ha! I only got a few years on you, so watch that teasing. Gotta admit though, my bum legs don't appreciate all the bending and kneeling some days, but I like to stay busy, you know."

"I know. Things have been rather slow at the paper, haven't they? It's been weeks since Mr. Quigsby assigned you a story."

"I checked in with Morty the other day to see if he'd forgotten about me, but it's just the summertime slump. When it gets hot, everyone takes a break from crime and other newsworthy shenanigans. Ain't even been any good ghost sightings," I joked.

"Let's keep it that way. I know you like to pretend you're a skeptic, but I've had quite enough of unexplained goings-on, thank you very much!"

I had to agree with Victoria there. Back in the spring, I'd had a mysterious conversation with a teenage boy dressed up as an angel only to find out he'd passed away prior. I'd never believed in spiritual stuff before, but it was hard to explain away what happened to me as anything other than a ghostly visitation, like that guy Scrooge gets in the old Christmas tale. Only I hadn't learned much of a lesson from it other than there are some awful evil and cruel people in the world, and that was a lesson I'd been taught long ago.

"That reminds me," Victoria said. "I got a letter from Mrs. Hasselwhite. She wanted to let us know Lily was doing much better and even sent a picture."

She drew a snapshot out from her pocket of a smiling girl with long blonde braids, holding the leash of a tiny terrier dog that was looking up at her worshipfully. Lily was the little sister of the aforementioned angel. Victoria and I had thought briefly we might adopt her for our own before finding out her mother was alive and helping reunite the two.

"She seems pretty happy, don't she?" I said. "Looks as though she got a pet to take Archie's place."

"Speak of the Devil." Victoria laughed, as our resident black cat jumped up on the bench beside us. He'd lost a leg during some of the brouhaha with Lily, but it didn't seem to bother him none once it healed up. Though I did catch him sniffing where it used to be from time to time like he was puzzled about what went with it.

"Must have heard his name." I stroked the animal's sleek fur as he thrummed in satisfaction. "What you got there, buddy boy?"

Archie spit out an unusual looking feather, mottled white and black. I picked it up with trepidation. "Not more feathers. We've had enough of that."

"Agreed!" Victoria said, grabbing the feather and throwing it over her shoulder. "After all our excitement, I think we can appreciate a nice boring summer day, can't we?"

No sooner said than we heard the hum and scrape of a motorbike coming up the gravel driveway. The bike ground to a halt in front of us. The rider pulled off a beat-up leather helmet and pair of driving goggles to reveal none other than old Maudie Adams, a fellow reporter at the Crier.

"Put it in gear, Malhaven," she yelled. "We got a big story breaking. Murder, and the boss wants you on it!"

So much for a boring summer day.

CHAPTER TWO

"*M*urder!" Victoria exclaimed. "Who? Where?"

"I know the where. The who and the why is what we gotta find out," Maudie said. With her signature turban of iron-gray hair smashed flat to her head by the helmet, she looked even more eccentric than usual, but there was no missing her satisfaction.

I couldn't blame her. We didn't have many murders in Carsworth City, so I'm sure the reporters in the bullpen would've been fighting over this one. I wondered why Morty assigned it to me. I usually got the oddball stories, which of late had meant ghost sightings among other unusual happenings.

"What's the deal?" I asked.

"All I know so far is it's at the Royale," she said, mentioning the town movie palace, "and we better get over there before anyone scoops us."

"Who's gonna scoop us? The Crier is the only game in town."

"Murder's always a big story. Bet some of the Chicago papers send someone down. We don't want those big city boys to show us up, do we?"

"Probably some lowlife stabbed in a brawl or something. The big papers ain't gonna bother with penny ante stuff like that."

"I dunno, Morty seemed awful excited about it, and you know he don't get excited about much."

That was certainly true. Morty was a man of few words and even fewer emotions. It poked my curiosity to know what had him worked up. "Guess we better check it out then. Why don't you jump in the Champ with me, and we'll go together?"

"No, thanks," said Maudie. "I'd rather travel my way than in that old rattle heap you call an automobile. I'll meet you there. I'm not on the case, but I ain't got nothing better to do. I can help you out."

Before I could discuss with her whether I agreed she'd be a help or not, she'd slammed her helmet and goggles on and was scooting back down the driveway the way she'd come in.

"You'd better run." Victoria gave me a little shove to get me up off the bench. "Maudie will have the whole thing figured out before you even get there."

"That'd save me a heckuva lot of trouble, wouldn't it?"

"Aren't you excited? I thought you were tired of working on human interest and gossip stories. This sounds like a chance to get back into the big time."

"Just wondering why Morty thought of me. Hope we don't find it's another ghost on the loose. Give me a plain old-fashioned gangland assassination any day."

"Well, if you don't get going, you'll never find out!"

"Okay, okay, Mrs. J. If I didn't know better, I'd think you were trying to get rid of me."

"Never." And she planted a big one on my kisser to prove it, sending me off with an idiotic grin on my face.

I jumped into my Studebaker Champion, giving it a fond pat on the steering wheel. I was still smarting from Maudie's comment. The Champ might not be much to look at, but it was paid for and got me everywhere I needed to go. What more did you want from a car?

The cemetery ain't far outta town, so it wasn't long until the farms and fields of the countryside gave way to the brownstones and traffic lights of our fair city. The Royale Moving Picture Palace, as the big, old-fashioned sign all lit up in lights declared, wasn't too far from the newspaper's offices downtown. There was quite a crowd gathered. The cops had cordoned off the street, so I had to park a block away and hoof it.

I shoved through the gawkers in time to find my buddy Flanagan arguing with a determined-looking Maudie in front of the theater's box-office.

Joey gave me the eye. "And now here's the Crier's high-society reporter. What are they doing? Turning the whole office out onto the streets today?"

Brushing off the crack, I got right to the point. "Who's dead and how, when, why, and where?"

"You want me to do all your work for ya? You pride yourself on your investigative skills. Why don't you investigate?"

"Whataya think I'm doing? What's with the hard guy act?"

"This is a murder investigation, Jimmy. I ain't got time to babysit a bunch of scribblers."

"C'mon, Joey. You know I been itching to get back to serious reporting. This is my chance. If I mess it up, Morty might think I'm all washed up with the big stories. Whataya say, pal. For old times' sake."

"You gonna start blubbering in a minute?" Flanagan asked. "This ain't just a big deal for you. It's a big case for me, and I ain't gonna blow it. Now you and Miss Maudie here can go wait outside the barriers with the rest of the hoi-polloi. If I'm feeling generous, I may come out and make a statement to the press later on."

I was kinda floored, I'll admit. I could usually count on Joey to keep me in the loop. Made me think there was more to all of this than met the eye if he was being so cagey, which only made me more curious. However, there seemed nothing for it but to retreat in mortification as some of the boys in blue smirked at us. Most of the cops I knew liked nothing better than to lord it over the rest of us mere mortals, so they were enjoying seeing us booted by their boss.

Maudie grabbed ahold of my sleeve and started dragging me away as we melted back into the crowd. "Don't mind that jerk. I know another way in."

"What—to the theater? I dunno. Joey's still a pal. I don't want to get him in bad with his captain."

She shot me a look of pure disgust. "Are you kidding me? What kind of a reporter do you call yourself? It's all about the story. I'm going with or without you. If you wanna go back to the paper and explain to Morty you didn't have the nerve to follow me, go right ahead."

Maudie marched off, leaving me with a dilemma. Imagining the blasting Morty would give me if I came back without a story, I found my feet following after her before I knew what I was about. She shuffled around the building next door to the theater. It had an Italian restaurant on the first floor and cheap apartments above. Bet they got the smell of marinara sauce up there. Might not be so bad come to think of it. Sorry, my brain works that way sometimes. Where was I?

Oh, yeah. I followed Maudie around the building to an alley. We had to clear a path through a bunch of old wooden crates and some garbage I'd just as soon not look close enough at to identify. We made it to the back of the building where there was a fire escape clinging to the side.

"You grab it," Maudie commanded, pointing at the spring-loaded escape ladder. "You're tall enough if you give it some oomph."

She was right. I had to take a running jump and barely got off the ground with my bum legs, but I was able to get a hand around the retracted ladder and pull it down to the ground.

"Ladies, first."

She grunted but made short work of scooting up the rungs. I climbed up after, averting my eyes, being a gentleman and having no inclination to see what kind of knickers she had on under her skirt. My weight kept the ladder in position until I got to the fire escape proper, but then it retracted with a bang that made us both start.

"Shhh," Maudie scolded me. "We don't want no nosy neighbors looking out here to see what we're up to."

"What *are* we up to?" I inquired.

She just kept climbing. Deciding I didn't have a lot to lose by taking her lead, I followed.

The fire escape took us up to the top floor but left us short of the roof.

"Now, what?" I asked.

"Now you give me a boost."

I'm a big guy, but Maudie was no lightweight. Sighing, I laced my fingers together. "Step on up."

It took some doing, but I finally got her over the top. By shimmying onto the fire escape railing and almost pulling my arms out of their sockets, I managed to pull myself over after her. She led me to the edge of the building.

"That's the movie house. All we gotta do is hop over." There was only about a three-foot gap between buildings, but I still held my breath to see Maudie take a flying leap. She landed with all the grace of a gazelle with broken ankles, but she made it. With my long legs, it was more a step than a leap for me. Once we were over there, I could see what she was aiming for. There was a bulkhead with a door to a stairwell that led down to the theater.

"How'd you know about this?" I asked Maudie.

"Me and my girlfriends used to sneak in to see the silent picture shows when we was young and broke. I liked the movies better before everyone started yakking. They could really act in those days. And the organist was a dreamboat. All the girls were in love with him. I can still see his mustache."

Hoping to cut short the trip down memory lane, I tried the handle of the door on the bulkhead expecting it to be locked, but it swung open toward me with no problem. No problem, that is, until I saw the body waiting for us just inside.

CHAPTER THREE

"Holy cow!" Maudie hollered. "Will you look at that!"

It was my turn to say shush, but it was too late. I heard voices down below and before we could beat a hasty retreat, a couple of plain clothes detectives rushed up the stairs, took in the scene, and reached for their handcuffs.

"Hey, Flanagan, looks like we found the bad guys!" one yelled down the stairs. "And get this, there's another stiff up here."

Before Maudie and I could protest our innocence, Joey appeared on the scene.

"You two! Didn't I tell you to scram? One of these days, Jimmy boy, your failure to take my advice is gonna get you in real trouble. How'd you even get up here without us seeing you? And who's your friend on the ground there?"

"Your guess is as good as mine," I protested. "We just arrived. Took a shortcut from the next building over."

"I see. Breaking in and just happened to turn up another body. That your story?"

"Hey, it's not our fault you didn't do a thorough search of the building. What've you guys been up to all this time?"

"We were getting to it. Why do you think Wilson and Fink were Mr. Johnny-on-the-spot to catch you in the act?"

"We saved you some trouble then. You oughta be thanking us."

Joey gave me a look. "I guess you're witnesses of a sort now. If I turn you away again, I have a feeling you'd just wiggle back in through the sewers like a couple of rats. Might as well come on in and join the party. Fink, you and Wilson fetch the doc and photo boys for our latest victim here."

I made to step over the impediment in the doorway when it suddenly gave out with a groan. We all jumped about a foot in the air.

Joey recovered first. "Didn't any of you guys check for a pulse?" he said, glaring around at us.

"Sorry, boss," Wilson mumbled. "Guess we got overexcited."

"I'll give you something to get excited about, but it can wait. Get the ambulance boys up here and check this guy for ID. For all we know, he's the killer. I'm surrounded by amateurs. You two, with me."

Maudie and I followed meekly enough, though I did try to get a glimpse of the guy on the ground. He had a cheap, gray suit, but his brown fedora had drifted down over his face, so I didn't get a chance to check out his looks none. Figured there'd be time for that later.

We charged down the stairs and landed in the control room for the theater. Most of it was taken up by two huge projectors that the operator switched between to keep the movie running without interruption as the film rolls ran out. There was other equipment sitting around. I had a buddy who'd worked at the Royale, so I knew some of it was for splicing and editing the film to add coming attraction trailers and newsreels.

It was hot and close in the booth, so I was glad to escape to the lobby and find out the air conditioning system they'd installed was running. The cool air attracted more customers in the summer than the movies did sometimes. It sure felt good to me. Our little adventure to get in the building had left me hot and bothered in more ways than one. The doc and ambulance guys hustled past us to check out the guy upstairs.

"Now that we're here, can you give us any info?" I asked Joey.

"Blake Brighton, manager, came in early to make sure the joint was all shipshape for the first matinee. Turns on the lights in the theater to check the ushers got everything cleaned up last night and notices a lady sitting in the first row. Calls out to her. No response. Comes to find she's a goner, but still sitting up in her seat with her handbag on her lap and a suitcase beside her."

"Don't suppose we could take a look?"

"Not this time, Jimmy. I know I've let you tag along to domestics and gangland killings, but I gotta feeling this is gonna be a weird case, and I wanna play everything by the book."

"But weird is my beat," I reminded him. "At least give us a cause of death."

"Don't know yet. No obvious wounds on the body. Doc'll have to take a closer look."

"Maybe it's natural causes," Maudie suggested.

"I was wondering that until we came across our friend upstairs. Now the plot thickens, as they say."

Maudie snorted. "Who says that?"

"Ain't you ever read a book, Maudie?"

"Not if I can help it. I get full up with words at the paper. I'm saving up for my own TV set but in the meantime, I go next door to my neighbor. I don't like her taste in programs, but beggars can't be choosers. Now that's a saying they do say!"

"You guys are as good a comedy act as Martin and Lewis," I said, "but this ain't helping with our investigation."

"My investigation, you mean," said Joey. "You two might as well get out of here and for good this—"

Flanagan was interrupted by the ambulance crew carrying out a stretcher followed by the doc. Maudie stepped back and bent over to look at something on the ground. I pushed forward for a better look at the unconscious patient. This time I saw the guy's face and almost wished I hadn't, though I'm hardly one to talk with my mangled kisser. I'd seen wounds like that before on men I'd served with in the war.

"Burns?" I asked the doc.

"Looks like it, but old ones. They've healed up about as good as they'll ever get, poor fellow."

"So, what's wrong with him?"

"Not sure yet. There were no obvious wounds, just as with the woman. I'll ride to the hospital with the man and hand him over to some of my colleagues for closer examination. The ambulance will come back for the woman, and I'll start an autopsy as soon as I've had some lunch. Never like to do an autopsy on an empty stomach," he added with sinister good cheer before scooting out to catch up with the ambulance team.

"What about ID?" Flanagan said to Fink and Wilson, who'd brought up the rear of the procession.

"Nothing obvious," said Wilson. "We checked all his pockets. Just a sawbuck and some loose change."

"What about the woman?" I asked. "Any clue who she is?"

Joey nixed that. "Enough, Jimmy. You already got more than you started with. Knowing your way with the blarney, I'm sure you can spin that straw into gold good enough for the sheep who read the Crier."

"That's a cheap shot, Joey, even for you. What's got into you today? Wake up on the wrong side of the bed again? Or maybe the wife did."

"What's that supposed to mean?" He had a look like he was two seconds from punching me in the kisser. We hadn't scrapped since we were kids, though we'd come close now and then. We always gave each other a hard time, but I must've struck a nerve. Made me wonder what was going on at home with his wife, Doreen. Maybe there was trouble in paradise.

"C'mon, Jimmy," Maudie said, tugging on my sleeve. "Don't bother the nice officer. Let's do as he says and scram."

I was gonna argue, but she gave me such a pinch, I'm surprised I didn't squeal like a baby. I may not have graduated top of my class, but even I could see she was excited about something and wanted a chance to tell me in private.

"Very well, Detective Flanagan," I said, giving him my best bow and a flourish of my fedora. "Your wish is our command."

Joey gave me a hard look to let me know he was still mad, but he let us walk out the front doors of the theater into the crowd of rubber-neckers without any more guff.

"What's the big idea?" I said to Maudie, rubbing my arm. "That's gonna leave a bruise."

"Look! It fell on the ground when they were carrying that guy away."

She opened her hand and there it was, a key with a room number and the words *Starlight Hotel* big as day. "I got us a hot lead!"

CHAPTER FOUR

"What're you doing, Maudie? That's evidence. Why didn't you turn it over to the cops?"

"They had their chance to search the guy. Fink and Wilson are total mooks. How stupid you gotta be to miss a clue like that? And why should I do their job for them? They weren't keen on helping us out none."

"That's different. Besides, how do you know it belongs to the guy? Coulda belonged to one of the ambulance crew or the doc."

"No way. I watched it fall out of the guy's hat when they was taking him away. Bet those two goons didn't even think to look there. Flanagan was right—amateurs."

"Still, we oughta go give it to Joey. It ain't right."

"Jimmy, when did you turn into such a sad sack? Is this the same guy led his platoon up those beaches in the South Pacific during the war? I say we go do a little investigating of our own. We can let Flanagan in on what we find out and make a big splash for the paper. It's a win-win for everyone."

"Maudie, hand me that key."

"No way! And if you try to take it, I'm gonna start screaming bloody murder. There's not one guy in this crowd who won't come to the defense of a poor little old lady like me against a tough with a face like yours, and you know it!"

"Little old lady." I snorted. "Viper more like it."

"You know I'll do it, so make your choice. Head back to the paper and write up the pitiful excuse for a story you got so far, or come along with me and see if we can't really get a scoop."

Faced with such a quandary, I did what any right-minded reporter would do and decided to follow the lead. I knew Maudie was a thousand times too stubborn to sway from the path once she'd chosen it. The least I could do was try and keep her out of trouble.

She must of could tell from my face that I'd given up the fight 'cause she turned tail and headed down the cross street that would bring us to the hotel. It was a place we reporters were all plenty familiar with, being the kind of rundown joint that was a hotbed of criminal activity. I'd covered plenty of low-rent hanky-panky of every variety there.

The buzzing neon sign hanging off the side of the building stayed lit up twenty-four hours a day, but the Ts in Starlight had given up the ghost a long time ago. There were a couple of shady-looking customers hanging out on the stoop who made themselves scarce when they saw us coming.

Maudie read out the number on the key. "Room 406. Fourth floor."

I grunted agreement as I opened the front door of the hotel for her. I might be irritated but I was still a gentleman. Some lessons my ma taught me, I won't ever forget. We headed for the stairs but were rudely interrupted.

"Where do you think you're going?"

We turned to find a dame at the front desk glaring at us. At first glance, I thought she was young, but as we got closer, I saw the bottle-blonde hair and pancake makeup were hiding a middle-aged dragon with a jaded look in her eye.

"Just visiting a friend," I said.

"What friend? Name?"

"He's in 406. Guy with the ugly face," Maudie volunteered.

"He went out. Haven't seen him come back yet."

"That's okay. We'll go wait for him."

"Not on my watch."

I had to laugh. "Since when does this fleabag joint keep such a close eye on anything that goes on here?"

"We're under new management: me. I'm trying to clean up the place and can't have strangers wandering around. You can wait here in the lobby if you like," she added, pointing to two poor excuses for armchairs shoved against one wall with a half-dead fern on a rusted metal stand between them.

I decided to try a little of my trademark Malhaven charm. "I'm Jim, and this here is my aunt."

The snort from Maudie didn't help my cause, but I soldiered on.

"And you are?" I asked, with a smile and a flash of my pretty gray eyes.

"Phoebe. Like the bird."

"What bird?" asked Maudie.

"The songbird, of course. Ain't you ever heard of a phoebe?" The woman gave her the evil eye.

I hastened to intervene. "What a lovely name! Your parents had excellent taste."

"That's not the name they gave me. They called me Maude if you can believe it. Ain't that an awful name? I changed it soon as I could. Who'd wanna be stuck with that all their life?"

I put a restraining hand on my "aunt's" shoulder, afraid she was about to blow her top, but I had to give it to her. She knew how to keep her cool when a story was at stake.

"Quite an odd name, Phoebe," Maudie said. "Suits you."

I could see the woman trying to work out whether that was a compliment and decided not to give her time to dwell on it.

"So, Phoebe, my aunt and I are here from out of town to visit my cousin. Seeing as we're family, I'm sure you won't mind if we wait upstairs in his room."

"Do you really think I'm that dumb, Mr. Malhaven?"

I never used the phrase "the jig is up" before, but I swear that's what flashed through my mind as I exchanged a glance with Maudie.

Phoebe laughed at us like we were the funniest thing she'd seen in a year. "You should see your faces. Think word doesn't get around about the big reporter with a scar who's always poking his nose in where he shouldn't? And my actual cousin, Wanda, down at the Automat pointed you out to me once, Maudie Adams. Said you were always causing trouble."

"That's a lie! Wanda's got a huge mouth. She can dish it out, but she can't take it. Hey, did you make up that story about your name?"

"Sure, wanted to see if I could get a rise out of you," Phoebe said with another belly laugh. "So now we're all being on the up and up, what're you two really doing here?"

Deciding that to confess all was the only strategy left to us, I explained our mission.

"Taken to the hospital? Hope that don't mean he ain't gonna be able to come back and settle up his bill."

"He'll be even less likely to if he's arrested for murder," I pointed out. "Maybe we can find something upstairs that'll clear him."

"Why not leave it to the cops? I could get in trouble for helping you out. What's in it for me?"

I been around the block enough times to recognize a prompt for a little flashing of the green. Unfortunately, I had a buck fifty in change in my pocket, if that. I gave Maudie a sheepish look. She sighed but opened up her voluminous black handbag and fished a fiver out of it.

"Jimmy's friends with a bigshot detective. He'll see you don't get in any hot water, but here's a little something to show our appreciation."

Phoebe tucked the five-spot into her cleavage and gave us the nod. "If the guy was up to date on his room, I might object, but given he only paid for one night and has been here five, with nothing but empty promises so far, I'll turn a blind eye. But do me a favor and don't take nothing and leave it like you found it, okay? The cops are bound to come nosing around sooner or later, and I don't need trouble."

"Scout's honor," I said.

"I didn't know you were a scout," said Maudie.

I poked her in the side. "C'mon."

"Hang on," she said, turning to Phoebe. "You must know the guy's name, right? Can you tell us, or do you need another bribe for that tidbit?"

"That one I'll gift you for absolutely nothing. It's John Doe."

CHAPTER FIVE

The looks on our faces earned us another of Phoebe's belly laughs.

"I thought you was trying to get things on the up and up here, but you're renting a room to someone with a phony name," Maudie complained.

"I wasn't born yesterday. I turned him away, but he showed me a passport. Had all kinda stamps from places he'd been. Said his parents had a sense of humor. Crossed my mind it was a forgery, but to tell you the truth, I felt kind of sorry for the guy. Can't be easy walking around in public with a face like that. Guess you know the feeling," she threw my way.

"Not me," I said with a wink. "I get a kick out of scaring women and babies."

She gave me a look that made me sorry I'd winked at her. "Now I see you close up, it ain't so bad. Gives you an air of danger. Lots of women go for that kind of thing, you know," she added with what I guess you'd say was a simper.

Maudie'd had about enough. "I can see where Wanda got all her charm. Must run in the family."

I gave Phoebe a smile and a hurried thanks, then hustled Maudie away and up the stairs before she had a chance to say anything else and ruin the all-clear from our hostess. When I made the mistake of looking behind us, Phoebe waggled her red-tipped fingers at me in a coy way that sent chills down my spine.

We reached the fourth floor, huffing and puffing. Maudie used the key to open the door to room 406.

"I hope we ain't gonna get blamed for this mess," she said.

The room looked as if a hurricane blew through, followed by a rampaging stampede of bulls like I seen in a newsreel story once from Spain. The cheap dresser mirror had been busted. The pieces lay winking all over the stuff on the floor. There was half-eaten food and wrinkled shirts and briefs. Copies of the Crier and some of the big city newspapers were draped around everywhere.

"Looks like our John Doe is fond of a crossword puzzle," I remarked, picking up one of the papers and seeing all the squares were neatly filled in black ink without a strikethrough in sight. "Don't make mistakes either."

"Must be some kinda genius. I can't never figure those things out and don't see the point in trying."

"I dunno. Can be a good way to pass the time on a stakeout."

"I'd rather eat. Looks like he was a fan of that too. But not such a fan of cleaning up after himself. Our songbird downstairs ain't gonna be happy to see this rat's nest, and look, ants!" Maudie cried with disgust, picking up an old banana peel. "Some people ain't fit to live in a pigsty."

"Maybe he had a lot on his mind. Must have had a hard life with his face. Those burns didn't happen last week. And that's just his face. We don't know about the rest of him. I had a couple of buddies go through it during the war. Burns are some of the worst pain you can imagine. When you're living with something as bad as that, might discourage you from caring about a lot of things."

"Yeah, looks like you're right about the pain. He's got a whole drugstore of pills here."

"That's not all," I added, holding up a syringe.

"Dope fiend?"

"Wouldn't be surprised. The docs give out morphine freely to burn victims in the hospital. Might be hard to kick the habit once they let you loose."

"So, maybe a veteran, burned in the war, drug addict, slob, but good penmanship and a brain if he's filled out all those crosswords right."

"Maybe. Though there's lotsa ways to get burns. Was hard to tell how old he was. Might have been too old for service."

"Nah, didn't you get a good look at his hands when they carried him out, Jimmy? Those weren't the hands of an old man. Bet you didn't notice the wedding ring, neither."

"You're one up on me there, Maudie. I gotta admit I was too busy taking in his mangled mug to notice, but that's pretty interesting. What if the stiff in the theater is, or was, his wife? Ninety percent of the time seems like it's the husband responsible when the wife turns up dead."

"But don't forget, he wasn't in such good shape when we stumbled across him. Maybe whoever killed her was trying to off him too."

"I dunno. Now that I think of it, our friend Phoebe didn't mention him having a roommate up here. The sharp eye she's keeping on the comings and goings, seems like she'd have noticed."

"Didn't Flanagan say they found a suitcase with her? Maybe she just got into town, and they met up at the theater."

"Why not meet here? Wouldn't that make more sense?"

"People don't always gotta make sense, do they, Jimmy? Half the trouble in this world is people not making any sense. I was saying to my neighbor Mildred only the other day that everyone seems like they gone crazy when you watch the news. I don't guess meeting up with your husband at the movie theater instead of his hotel is so strange. There's probably a perfectly logical explanation."

"Which is it? Does it not make any sense because it doesn't have to, or is there a sound reason for it?"

"Why do I have to do all the guesswork? You got a brain, don't you? Use it!"

"Yes, ma'am," I said with a grin. "But I need something more to work with. Let's keep looking around. We don't need to worry about making a mess since there already is one, but maybe we should try to leave things as they were as much as possible. Don't want to throw Flanagan any curve balls."

"You give him too much credit. I know you feel like you're brothers since you were brought up running around in the old neighborhood together, but he went his way and you've gone yours. You ain't on the same side anymore."

"Since when? Cops ain't our enemy."

"You just ain't paying attention. Sure, they don't hassle a mug like you, but there's plenty of people in this town could tell you stories about being roughed up or held overnight for no reason. Guys join the force 'cause they enjoy having power and pushing people around and no one can stop 'em. They ain't gonna investigate or turn against their own."

"It ain't like that. Flanagan may be tough on criminals, but he's fair. There's always gonna be a few bad apples, but a lot of the guys just want to help out. Keep the city safe so ladies like you can walk around unmolested. Protect shopkeepers from theft. Catch killers so they don't go free and off someone else. What's wrong with that?"

"Nothing, if it was all they did, but that ain't the way it is, Jimmy. Ask your friend Q. They roughed him up good for a phony charge back in the springtime before they let him go without even an apology."

I couldn't argue with that. Our resident researcher and now part-time photographer and reporter, Marquis Sutherland, had been falsely accused by a white girl of petty theft. The weight of the hammer that came down on him from the boys in blue had more to do with his skin color than the seriousness of the charge. Luckily, he'd been freed quickly, but it didn't undo the treatment he'd received. It made things a little awkward between us, what with Flanagan being my best friend. I've always been loyal to a fault, but it's hard when you feel like you're walking a tightrope between pals from opposite sides of the fence.

I tried to make it up to Q by talking the Crier's publisher into giving him a chance as a photographer and reporter. Louis Carsworth prided himself on his progressive views. It didn't take much to convince him to promote Q so he could pat himself on the back for "giving one of the oppressed minority a chance, just as an experiment, you know" as he put it to me.

I left that part out when I reported back to Q. He was excited to get a shot but was prepared to meet resistance from the other reporters on the paper. Most of them just ribbed him a bit like we all did with each other, but I'd seen enough side-eye to know not everyone appreciated Carsworth's "experiment."

It would've been useful to have Q with us. He was an ace photographer and could've got some pictures of the room to look at later in case we missed anything. As it was, we did the best we could sorting through the mess. I was turning over some of the debris on the ground with the eraser end of the pencil I always carried with me, when I noticed something interesting. A small photograph like you get when you cram into one of those photo booths at the carnival with your best girl.

Handsome-looking couple was my first impression. It was only when I looked more closely that I got a shock. Staring back at me was a very familiar face. In fact, it was the one I knew best in all the world. One Victoria Jankowski.

CHAPTER SIX

efore I could fully process the thought, the photo was snatched out of my hand.

"Hey, that looks a lot like your girl—"

"Fiancée," I corrected automatically, stunned at my discovery.

"That's funny, ain't it? They say we all got a double somewhere in the world, don't they? Is there anything written on it?"

I pulled it out of her hand and turned it over. It was blank. About as blank as my brain. I didn't try to correct Maudie, but if it wasn't Victoria Jankowski staring up at me from that photo, I'd eat my beloved hat, the same hat that had belonged to her late husband. I hadn't spent so many hours staring into those stormy blue eyes and memorizing every little wave in her honey hair not to know her when I saw her. She was definitely younger in the picture, late teens to around twenty I guessed.

"Probably the guy, don't you think?" Maudie said, pointing to the man in the photo. "John Doe, before he got scorched."

"Could be, I guess, but we shouldn't jump to conclusions. Could be anyone. Could be someone else dropped this here."

"I guess you're right, but I'm thinking it's the guy. Handsome, too. What a shame. Do you think the dame is the woman at the movie palace? Husband and wife maybe. A little domestic quarrel. Might explain the state of this room. The broken mirror."

"And then what, ran off to the movies, her with a suitcase?"

"Maybe it's one of those 'other woman' deals. She threatens to tell the wife, and he has to off the girlfriend or the wife, one or the other. Whataya think, Jimmy?"

I didn't know what to think, but before I had a chance to answer, there was a knock at the door and it swung wide open. Phoebe stuck her head in, breathing hard with a harassed look on her face.

"Cheese it. The cops are on their way up."

We could hear the heavy tread on the stairs, too close to give us time to scoot. Flustered, I tucked the snapshot into the band of my hat, making sure it was tucked out of sight before plopping the fedora back on my head just as Flanagan, Fink, and Wilson pushed Phoebe aside and burst into the room.

"So, that's what the hurry was," Joey said. "Wondered why this dame took off up the stairs like a racehorse when I announced we was interested in room 406. I guess I should've known, but I'm still disappointed. What're you doing here, and how did you know where to come?"

"It's a hell of a coincidence, ain't it, Jimmy?" Maudie said, prompting me for back-up.

"Um, yeah," was the best I could do under the circumstances.

Maudie expounded. "We happened to find the key to this hotel room and being honest citizens, thought we'd come along and return it to its owner. Found the door open and the room in quite a state. We was gonna go back down and let the manager know she might want to call the police in and here you are. Now, I call that good timing, don't you, Detective Flanagan?"

Joey snorted. "Do you think police interference is a joke? I could arrest you both now and you wouldn't have a leg to stand on."

"I don't know. Finding and returning a hotel key ain't a crime that I know of, and Jimmy here has friends in high places with lots of money. Might not appreciate your casting uncalled for aspersions at him."

"Uncalled for aspersions, is it? What'd you do, Maudie? Invest in an encyclopedia set? And what have you got to say for yourself, Jimmy? You're being awful quiet."

Not able to formulate much of a useful thought since the jolt of finding Victoria's photo, I settled on, "What she said," which didn't exactly soothe Joey's feelings.

"What she said. So, you're both gonna play the joker, are you? Well, I've learned my lesson. Search 'em, boys."

Fink and Wilson exchanged glances. I think they were trying to figure out if they'd rather pat down the six-four gorilla or the old lady. Fink finally went for Maudie and Wilson came for me. Tried to slow down my heartbeat so it wasn't so loud. I was counting on the fact they wouldn't do any more thorough a search on us than they had on the guy at the theater. I was relieved when Wilson didn't even take the hat off my head to see if I had something hidden under it, much less examine the liner and band.

It took Fink longer, mainly because he had to go through Maudie's purse, which seemed to contain every object known to man, but in the end, all they had to show for it was the key to the room, which they knew we had anyway.

"That's it, boss," Fink reported.

"Okay," said Joey. "I want you two out of here. And if I find you one more place you shouldn't oughta be today, I'm locking you both up for obstruction."

"What about the guy at the hospital?" I asked.

Wilson jumped in to answer before Flanagan could stop him. "They think he overdosed on something. Probably morphine or heroin. They were able to bring him around enough to tell us where he was staying, though it's touch and go with him the docs say. And get this, his name is—"

"John Doe," said Maudie. "We're way ahead of you. What about the girl?"

"You're so smart, you figure it out," growled Joey. "Now out with the both of you. And leave the real investigating to the professionals. No more breaking and entering, got it?"

I grabbed Maudie by the arm and ushered her away before she

could argue and antagonize Joey any more than he already was. I thought he'd gotten over being sore at me for letting some vigilante justice rob him of his last murder suspect back in the spring, but I was getting the impression it still smarted. He'd had a lot of explaining to do to his superiors, so I couldn't blame him since he had a wife and pension to think of.

That reminded me of how angry Joey had got earlier over my crack about Doreen. I used to eat dinner with them most Sundays, but since Victoria and I had been together, I'd gotten out of the habit. Made me feel like I hadn't been the best friend if I didn't even know the state of their marriage. Maybe when we both had less on our minds, I'd check in with him. Give him a shoulder to cry on if he needed one.

But for now, my mind was too full of the photo I'd found. I was in two minds whether to rush home and show it to Victoria or not. It might be a shock if someone she knew or who had known her husband was mixed up in some funny business, and Victoria had weathered more shocks in her life than most people. It wasn't long ago that her twin sister had been murdered by their own mother no less. I hated to be the one to present her with another blow.

I was wracking my brains to think how the picture might have ended up in the room. Was the guy an old boyfriend of hers? She'd never mentioned anyone but Lukasz to me, and as she'd lived at the Sisters of Mercy orphanage until she got married, I didn't think she'd had much opportunity for running around. Who else could he be?

And then it hit me. Bryant Bellingham, Victoria's half-brother. He'd been engaged to her twin sister, Janice, which is a whole other story, but Janice and Victoria had looked as alike as two peas in a pod. Maybe Bryant had finally come to visit and brought along a picture of Janice when she was younger to show Victoria.

Victoria had tried to get in touch with him more than once, but he'd been cagey about visiting. We couldn't blame him none, given the unusual circumstances of his birth and the shocking true identity of his fiancée, but we'd never gotten any indication he was suffering from burn wounds. It could explain his reluctance to meet with her. Maybe he was ashamed.

The timing didn't seem quite right. Those burns looked old, and no one had ever mentioned Bryant being injured. Janice had seemed a superficial kind of girl, not the type who would've fallen for someone she couldn't show off to all her friends like some kind of prize. But it would explain the photo.

"You gonna go to the paper and write this up?" asked Maudie when we made it back out to the front stoop of the hotel.

"By rights, you should. You've done most of the legwork today. I was just along for the ride."

"You know Morty won't go for that. When he assigns a story, he expects you to write the story. What's bothering you? Are you worried about Flanagan? He'll get over it."

"No, it's the photo."

"What—you're not thinking that's really your girl, are you?"

"Her, or her twin. They looked an awful lot alike you know."

"So do lots of other gals with her coloring. But if you're worked up about it, why not run home and show it to her? I saw you squirrel it away in your hat. Smart thinking, but now who's withholding evidence, eh, big guy? Anyway, you'd still have time to get back to the paper and knock out a couple of columns before deadline. I seen how fast you type."

"I don't want to upset her."

"Pssh, that lady is tough as nails. You might as well learn now she won't thank you for trying to protect her. Women like that want to be treated as an equal. Better not to get married if you're gonna try and keep things from her."

I knew Maudie was right. Victoria had never asked me to sugarcoat the truth and never would. Looked as if there was nothing for it, but to show her the photo for my own peace of mind. I could only hope I wouldn't be trading mine for hers.

CHAPTER SEVEN

It was an anxious drive for me back out of town. I'd worked myself into quite a state by the time I drove up the cemetery's long gravel driveway and parked in front of the main house. I seen right away that Victoria's red Caddy convertible was missing. Can't say there wasn't a part of me that was relieved to have an excuse to put off showing her the picture a while longer.

I wandered into the mansion to see if anyone knew where she'd gone. Came across Mr. Cressley vacuuming the dining room carpet. He was technically master of the house since marrying Victoria's Aunt Livinia, but even that haughty dame was out of luck when it came to convincing him to give up his household chores, including cleaning and cooking some of the finest meals you can get outside of a fancy French restaurant. My feeling was some guys ain't cut out for sitting around with their feet up, and Cornelius Cressley was one of them.

He saw me coming and turned off the vacuum with a smile of greeting. Cressley don't talk after having suffered an unfortunate incident at the hands of some gangsters back in Prohibition days, but he makes himself understood.

"Victoria?" he mouthed at me.

"Yeah, I was hoping to have a word with her, but I see her car's gone."

He nodded and pulled out the notebook and fancy gold pen he kept on him at all times, scribbling me out a note in his elegant handwriting.

She and Mrs. Cressley went to the Board of Directors meeting at Sisters of Mercy. Back late afternoon.

That made sense. They'd both wrangled seats on the Board after Victoria had found out it was all men with some very old-fashioned ideas about who was fit for adopting some of the poor orphans at Sisters of Mercy. Victoria was there for reform. Liv just liked to put her two cents in wherever she could. I pitied the men who had to wrangle with those ladies. They were both formidable in their own way.

I gave Cressley the nod and a vote of thanks before heading to the kitchen to make myself a sandwich. I wasn't feeling so hungry after the upset of finding the photo, but I'm a big guy who'd found out it was usually a mistake to miss a meal. Livinia griped constantly about how much money it took to keep me fed, but I figured since I provided a lot of free labor around the boneyard, I earned my share of the larder.

Decided after my meal that I might as well head back into town and see if I could dig up any more dirt before writing my story. I took a detour on the way to the car to stop by the small gravestone of Karolina Jankowski. I knew Victoria still visited it every day. I'd seen her there often enough. There was even a smooth spot worn away from where she'd laid her hand so often in benediction on top of the little lamb that decorated the monument to her daughter's memory.

I picked a pink rosebud on the way and lay it on top of the small grave. I'd often tried to imagine what Victoria went through in those dark days. First finding out her husband had been killed in the war. Then giving birth with no relatives to comfort her. And finally, those few short months she'd had with Karolina before that fragile spirit had been snuffed out. Enough to make most women turn sour, but not Victoria. She'd weathered those storms, and others almost as bad since. While she felt them deeply, I'd never seen any quit in her.

That she'd been willing to give me a chance made me one of the luckiest men alive. She'd loved Lukasz and her little girl with all her heart but somehow, she had enough room left over in there for a big lug like me. I couldn't wait to see her walking down the aisle toward me on our wedding day, and I sure didn't want any murder investigation to get in the way or spoil it for us.

I thought over what to do next as I drove back into town. Joey had made it clear I wasn't welcome poking my nose into police business, and I figured me and Maudie had tried his patience enough for one day, so I headed to the paper to check in with Q. He had a good head on his shoulders and had more than once helped me figure out a big story. Maybe he'd have a bright idea about another angle we could pursue.

His promotion to part-time reporter hadn't come with the gift of a desk and typewriter in the reporter's bullpen. I'd offered to share mine, but I think he preferred his privacy down in the basement morgue where the paper kept all its back issues. He'd worked hard on organizing everything and stocking up on reference materials so we didn't have to trek over to the town library so often. I'll also be the first to admit some of the other reporters hadn't exactly made him feel welcome upstairs.

I bypassed the newsroom, not wanting to catch Morty's eye in case he wanted an update on my story. Found Q downstairs at one of the big tables with a whole pile of books spread out in front of him.

"Whatchu up to?" I asked.

"Oh, hello, Mr. Malhaven," he said, looking up and sliding his glasses back into place on his nose.

"I thought we agreed on Jim or Jimmy now we're both newshounds?"

"I'm sorry, it just doesn't feel right."

"I know, I know. Respect your elders and all that. You make me feel like an old, old man sometimes, Q. Or maybe I should start calling you Mr. Sutherland. That would only be fair. But what's with all the books," I said, laying my hat on the table and taking a seat opposite him.

"I'm doing some background research for a story."

"Something for the Crier?" I asked, lighting up a smoke.

"I guess I could show it to Mr. Quigsby, but I doubt he'd run it."

"Morty'll run anything if he thinks it'll sell papers. What's it all about?"

"A lynching down in Georgia. Two young couples were pulled from a car on the Moore's Ford bridge. One of the women was even pregnant, but they were shown no mercy. They were all shot and killed by a mob of white men."

"Sounds familiar. The summer after the war ended, right? I remember one of the guys was a veteran. Served in the Pacific like me. There was a lot in the news about it at the time, but I don't remember what came of it all."

"Nothing. The FBI was sent in to investigate and a grand jury was called, but they declared there wasn't enough evidence to bring charges against anyone. None of the witnesses was willing to identify any of the killers. It's coming up on five years since it happened. I thought I'd write up a story. If the Crier won't run it, maybe one of the big city papers will pick it up. I'd love to get people interested in the case again. Maybe finally see justice done."

"You sound like those crusading reporters they show on the TV. What's that program called? *The Big Story*. Maybe they'll be talking about you one day on there. You put me to shame with my little penny ante stuff."

"I heard you got assigned a big one this time though. Murders don't happen every day in this town. How's your investigation going?"

I filled him in on the mischief Maudie and me had gotten up to and made no secret of the fact Flanagan was not a fan of our meddling.

"Leaves me wondering what to do next," I said. "Normally, I'd go down to the station and pump some of the boys for information, but I think Joey was serious about tossing me in a cell if he sees my face one more time today."

Q couldn't hide a sour expression at mention of the cops, and I can't say I blamed him. When a fine upstanding citizen gets pulled in and roughed up on account of a trumped-up charge, it leaves them with a healthy skepticism of our boys in blue.

"And you didn't find anything of interest in the hotel room?" was all he said though.

I fidgeted a bit. Stubbed out my cig and lit another one. I was afraid Q wouldn't approve of my pilfering evidence and didn't know what he would make of Victoria's picture, but he'd proven on many occasions I could trust him, so in the end, I reached over and pulled the photo out of my hat.

"Just this," I said, handing it to him.

"Nice-looking couple. The lady resembles Mrs. Jankowski a bit, doesn't she?"

"More than a bit, I'd say, and it's got me hot and bothered. I was thinking maybe it could be a snapshot of her sister, Janice. They looked so much alike, they fooled everyone when they switched places."

"Either way, it does seem a strange coincidence, but the easiest way to find out would be to ask her, wouldn't it?"

"Yeah, I'm gonna next time I see her. But in the meantime, you got any bright ideas to help an old man out?"

"I know exactly what we should do. We should infiltrate the morgue."

CHAPTER EIGHT

"Huh?" I asked. "Ain't we in the morgue already? Why we gotta break in?"

Q cracked one of his quiet smiles. "Not the newspaper morgue. The real morgue. You know, the kind with bodies. One of my uncles works there."

"Janitor?" I suggested without thinking, then was sorry when I saw the look on Q's face.

"No. Actually, he's the head mortuary assistant. He helps the doctors perform autopsies and prepares the bodies for handing off to funeral homes. He had to go to Chicago to complete a course to get qualified."

"Sorry, Q, I didn't mean…"

"I know what you meant. You're not the first person to make assumptions when I tell them about Uncle Cyrus. The point is, I have an in at the morgue. Maybe we can find out something about the woman they found in the theater."

"I dunno. I'd hate to get your uncle in any hot water."

"No one will think anything of it. I go visit him there all the time. The staff are used to seeing me around."

"Too bad you can't hide me in your pocket. I'm afraid I got a memorable mug."

"I'll go in first and scout around. If there's too many people, I'll gather whatever info I can and bring it back to you."

"Guess that's as good a plan as any. Can't think of anything else to do, and as it is, my story for the paper is gonna be pretty slim. If I could beef it up with a description of the woman or cause of death, it would make Morty a lot happier."

I drove us over to the hospital and hung around out back near the basement entrance while Q checked to see if the path was clear. It wasn't too many minutes before he stuck his head out and waved me in.

It was quiet and dark down there. Can't blame anyone for not wanting to hang around with a bunch of dead people if they don't have to. Q ushered me through a set of swinging steel doors at the end of the hallway and introduced me to his uncle, a tall man, big as me with salt and pepper hair and a ready smile.

"How do you do, Mr. Malhaven? Marquis has told me quite a bit about your adventures together. Reporting must be a very interesting profession."

"It has its moments, though most of it is pretty routine stuff, Mr. —?"

"Cyrus will do."

"Then call me Jim. I can never convince Q to use it. He says it's not right to be so casual with someone of my advanced years."

The big man laughed. "My sister brought him up right. But we better get to business. Marquis says you're interested in the woman they found at the theater. I don't mind showing you if you promise to be respectful, but we should hurry. I'm expecting Dr. Chambers soon to get started on the autopsy, and he doesn't allow an audience."

"I don't want to get you into any trouble."

"Oh, we get a lot of lookie-loos down here one way and another. You have a better excuse than most. At least you're trying to help the woman, aren't you? Q said you were investigating her death."

"I'm always interested in bringing killers to justice, if there is a killer. Sounds like the doc wasn't sure about cause of death though."

"He said there was no obvious cause when he stopped by earlier. The autopsy should give more information."

"Could be natural then."

"Could be, though she looks to be a young woman, so sudden death would be unusual. Come see."

He led us over to the middle gurney of three that all held a sheet-draped body. He gently pulled the sheet away so we could see the woman in question. I'd seen plenty of dead bodies before, both during and after the war, but it still always hits me to see the candle of life snuffed out. Somehow, they seem smaller and more diminished than you imagine they must have been in life.

The woman looked peaceful and certainly young. Maybe mid-twenties though it's hard to tell sometimes. The face tends to smooth out and relax in death. She was dressed in a gray suit with a pink blouse. Not the fanciest quality, but neat and clean. Her brunette hair was cut in a pageboy style, and she wore no makeup I could see, though she had a natural prettiness to her features. She was wearing stockings and a plain gray pump, but only one.

"Just one shoe?" I asked.

"That's all she had on when they brought her in. The other might have been left at the theater or dropped somewhere along the way. The ambulance men can be careless sometimes. She also had these."

He showed us a gray leather handbag and a simple hat with a gray net veil.

"Anything in the bag?"

"Haven't opened it yet. I imagine the police took a look to see if there were any identification cards. Dr. Chambers prefers me to wait to undress the body and go through any belongings until he arrives. We make a careful search and inventory together."

"She had a suitcase too, I heard."

"They probably took it back to the station to examine. We usually only deal with the clothing and accessories the victim was wearing in case it helps identify cause of death."

I looked at the woman's hands. "No gloves?"

"Not when they brought her in. Might be in her handbag. Women often take them off when they're inside."

"Looks like a wedding ring," I said, pointing to a narrow gold band, "but it's on the right hand."

Q spoke up. "In some cultures, it is common to wear it on the right hand rather than the left. For instance, Russia and some other eastern European countries."

"Interesting. Maybe she ain't American then. The guy they took out was wearing a wedding ring, so Maudie said. She didn't say which hand, but they were carrying him out headfirst, which means from where we were standing, she'd probably have been looking at his right hand. I'll have to see if she remembers. Any idea what color her eyes are?"

Cyrus put on a rubber glove and pulled back one eyelid gently. "Brown."

I took out my notepad and made a few notes, trying to record the look of the clothes, handbag and hat as best I could. Cyrus was covering the body back up when the doors slammed open, and Chambers bustled in.

"Visitors, Cyrus? You know I can't abide being watched while operating."

"Yes, Doctor. They were just leaving."

The doc gave me a good look. "I saw you this morning with the police, didn't I? At the movie theater. Are you investigating this young woman's death?"

"Yes," I said, since in a manner of speaking I was.

"Well, tell Detective Flanagan I'll send a full report along as soon as we're done here as usual. He should know by now I don't allow any outsiders to observe."

I crossed my fingers behind my back. I'm not above a little white lie now and again in pursuit of a story. I just hoped Q and Cyrus would go along with it.

"I'm looking to find out what's in the purse in case anything was missed earlier. Maybe I could stay for that?"

"Hm, we do usually start by going through any accessories. Cyrus, do you have a report started?"

"Yes, sir," he replied, picking up a clipboard with a stack of papers attached to it and a pen.

"Very well, we'll go through the contents of the purse for this officer, but then you and—who is this?" the doc asked, noticing Q.

"My nephew, Dr. Chambers. He dropped by with a message from his mother for me. Tell Dorothea I'll be happy to come over for Sunday dinner, Marquis."

"Yes, sir," Q said, taking the hint and making himself scarce. Better for Cyrus for us not to seem to be in cahoots, in case Chambers discovered I was a reporter and not a cop.

"Let's see what we have here," said the doc. "Pair of woman's gloves, gray leather, size six, small hands. Three dollars and forty-three cents in change. Train ticket from New York to Chicago. Small key with the number 78 on it—train station locker possibly? Photograph of man and woman. Interesting. The woman in the photo is not our woman, unless she was wearing a wig. Long, blonde hair."

He held the photo up in the air in front of my nose. "The man is quite handsome and the woman equally so, don't you think?"

My heart sank. It was the twin to the photo I'd found at the hotel.

CHAPTER NINE

$\mathcal{N}$ot quite a twin, I saw when I looked closer. The couple had changed their positions slightly, like you do in those booths where you get four chances at a photo. In this one, she had her head laid on his shoulder and was looking up at him with affection. It wasn't quite as clear a picture of the woman as the one I had, but I worried it would be enough for Flanagan to see the resemblance to Victoria.

"Perhaps you want to take the key and photo along to the station? They might help in your investigation," the doc suggested.

My hand started reaching, tempted at the opportunity to hide the photo and pursue the train locker lead, but I caught Cyrus shaking his head slightly out of the corner of my eye. He was willing to bend the rules in order for me to observe, but he wasn't about to let me walk out of there with evidence. He'd been more than fair, and I didn't want to get him in hot water after he'd helped me out.

"That's okay, Doc. I got some other leads to follow. Send the stuff along with the report."

"Very well. Now I will ask you to leave. We must start the undress-ing, and even the dead deserve as much modesty as we can grant them, especially the ladies," he added with a bit of a leer that didn't sit right with me since he was talking about a cadaver, but I just gave him and Cyrus a nod and took myself off.

I had no desire to see the poor girl split open, but I sure was curious to know what the cause of death was. She'd looked like it wasn't painful. I'd seen enough dead men's faces twisted up in agony to know that much. If anything, it looked like she was sleeping, the way she was lying there.

Q was waiting for me outside. I filled him in on what had happened.

"Another photograph?" he mused. "They must be from the same strip. I wonder why she would be carrying it around unless the woman was a friend or family member."

"Maudie was suggesting maybe it was a case of another woman. Maybe our victim found the photo and wanted to confront hubby about it?"

"So, are we assuming the man in the photo is the man at the theater before he was burned? And the victim was his wife? Maybe they got into an argument. He accidentally killed her then was overcome with remorse and tried to kill himself."

"I guess so. But that still leaves the how. We'll have to wait for the autopsy. It bothers me he was found at the exit at the top of the stairs. Looked more like he was trying to escape without attracting any attention but was overcome somehow. Unless of course, there's a third person involved that we ain't run across yet who attacked both of them."

"Do you think anyone will realize the woman in the photo resembles Mrs. Jankowski?"

"I wouldn't be surprised if Flanagan did. He's sharp, although her face ain't quite as clear as in the one I have."

"Maybe you should ask Mrs. Jankowski about it sooner rather than later. You wouldn't want the police to spring it on her without any warning."

"Good point, Q, but while we're here at the hospital, what say we see what's up with the guy they brought in? Flanagan said it looked like an OD. Touch and go. Depending on who they got guarding him, I might be able to get an update."

"You'd better go alone, Mr. Malhaven. I wouldn't be allowed on the white ward."

What a dope I am sometimes. I'd forgotten the wards were segregated. Q would stick out like a sore thumb. It wasn't the first time my thoughtlessness had left it up to him to point out something that should have been obvious to me.

I guess he could see I was flustered because he just said, "I'll go back to the paper. You can fill me in later," and turned to walk the five blocks back to the Crier on his own.

After sweet talking the receptionist in the hospital lobby, I headed upstairs and tracked down the right room. One of the jokers from earlier was on guard duty. Fink by name if not by nature.

"How's it going?" I asked, figuring I'd try the polite route first.

"What's it to ya?"

Not the most encouraging start, but I ain't easily discouraged.

"Just being civilized."

"Take the act somewhere else, Malhaven. The boss warned you to stay out of our business. Do you want me to report to him you was nosing around up here?"

"Do you want me to report to him how you and that Wilson mooch missed the key Maudie found at the theater? Don't exactly reflect well on your detecting skills."

"So you say. How do we know you didn't steal it off the guy before we got there?"

"You was on us like flies on honey. How'd we have time to search him? Unlike the pair of you, who had all the time in the world. Flanagan may be sore at me, but we're still pals from way back in the day. Who do you think he's gonna believe? You wanna take the chance?"

Fink tugged one finger on the tie around his neck like it was cutting off his air. "What's the big deal anyway? We found the hotel room with or without the key. For all the good it did us."

"Came up empty, huh?"

"Nothing but some clothes and stuff. No ID. Just a train ticket stub."

I almost asked if it matched the New York to Chicago ticket stub in the girl's purse before remembering I wasn't supposed to know about it.

"How's the guy doing?" I asked instead. "He up and talking?"

"Not so much. He woke up long enough to tell the boss about his hotel room, then passed out again. Wilson is sitting in there with him in case he lets spill with anything else, but mostly he's just mumbling in his sleep."

"Anything you can use?"

"Hard to say. Sounds foreign but nobody recognizes the lingo."

"Interesting. Maybe I could take a listen. I knew all kinda guys in the Army. Picked up a few words here and there. Might get lucky."

"Forget it, Malhaven. I already told you more than I should. As far as I'm concerned, we're all square. Now get out of here before the boss shows up and really gives you what for. He don't usually get that worked up, so I think he meant business about throwing you in a cell if he sees you again today."

"I think you might be right. Seemed a bit touchy. Trouble at home?"

"I wouldn't know. I'm not an *old pal* like some around here. Why you asking me?"

He had a point. If anyone should know why Joey was so wrought up about this case, it should be me. Fink wasn't the brightest bulb, but I decided he was right about making myself scarce before I was caught on the scene again.

I tipped my hat to him, which was more courtesy than the mook deserved, and made my way back to the Champ to head home and check in with Victoria before I wrote up my story. If the photo had nothing to do with her, it would make a great picture for the paper, since Maudie and I hadn't thought to take a camera to the theater. Readers go wild for that "can you help the police by identifying the couple in this photo" stuff. Makes them feel like they're private eyes on a case.

The drive went by quicker than I wanted. I had a natural reluctance to tackle Victoria with the snapshot. Whether it was her or her sister, it might rake up some past memory that wasn't a happy one. I'd rather she focused on the future with me and not rehash times gone by, but I knew that was selfish. I'd always played it as straight with her as I could, and now, when we were about to be husband and wife, was no sort of time to start keeping secrets.

I tracked her down in the kitchen, where she was putting a batch of cookies into the oven. She was a great one for baking, which was heaven for my taste buds but might be hell on my waistline if I wasn't careful.

"Hello, darling," she said with one of those megawatt smiles of hers that never got old.

I couldn't quite return it, and she noticed.

"Something wrong, Jim? What was the story about?"

"Dead woman at the Royale and a half-conscious guy who may or may not have offed her, if she was offed."

"How terrible either way. Was she very young?"

"Looked it."

"But that's not what's bothering you, is it?" she asked.

I decided to bite the bullet. The suspense was killing me. I pulled the photo out of my hat and passed it over to her.

"Why, Jim! Where on earth did you get this?"

"You recognize it?"

"Of course. It's me." She ran a finger over the man's face, tears brimming from her eyes. "And Lukasz. Oh, Lukasz."

CHAPTER TEN

That was a blow to the gut I wasn't expecting. I knew she'd only ever been with Lukasz before me, but I'd half convinced myself it was her sister Janice, and not Victoria, in the photo. To hear her confirm my worst fears was a lot to take in.

"I don't understand. How could you possibly have this?" she asked. "The last time I saw it was when Lukasz tucked it into his wallet before he went away to training camp."

"Lukasz," I repeated like a dope. "This is you and Lukasz?"

"Yes, we stopped at one of those photo booths when the carnival came to Farrelton the year we first met. You know, four poses for a quarter. We cut the strip in two and he took two with him and I kept the other two. I still have them. They're the only pictures I have of Lukasz. We couldn't afford a photographer for our wedding day and didn't have any friends with a camera. But how in the world is it here? I always assumed it… it went down…"

She didn't finish the thought, but she didn't have to. Lukasz had been serving aboard a Navy ship when it was torpedoed in the north Atlantic. She must've been picturing him sinking down into the ocean and taking the photo with him, if he wasn't blown up in the initial explosion that is. She'd told me the Navy was vague about the details, only confirming he wasn't among the survivors picked up by other ships in the area.

"You're positive it's the same picture?" I asked.

"Of course. I remember this dress so well. The cloth had these red cherry bunches all over it. I thought it was the prettiest thing I'd ever seen. It was a present from the nuns and one of the only non-uniform pieces of clothing I owned at the orphanage. Look at Lukasz. He looks so happy."

"Yeah, handsome guy. Guess I'm kind of a comedown for you."

She just gave me a look, and I gotta admit it wasn't the most appropriate time to be fishing for compliments.

"What year were these photos taken?" I asked.

"It was the summer of 1940. We got married that November, after my eighteenth birthday, and moved here to the cemetery when Lukasz got the caretaker position. We had a year together before he joined the Navy."

"He was drafted?"

"No. He'd registered, of course, but decided to volunteer after we heard the news about Pearl Harbor."

She looked at me with an uncertainty I don't often see from her. "I never told you. I didn't know how you would feel about it, but Lukasz was a pacifist. He had the gentlest soul of anyone I ever met. The idea of killing anyone was abhorrent to him, but he couldn't stand by and watch Americans be attacked without doing something. He was able to secure a spot as a medic so at least he felt like he would be helping people instead of hurting them. I hope that doesn't make you think less of him."

I didn't know what to think if I'm honest. I'd killed men in the war, but it was kill or be killed, or even worse, watch the men I lived and fought alongside of mowed down. We'd heard about conscientious objectors. Called them cowards or traitors or worse. It was hard to find sympathy for men who looked like they were trying to wriggle their way out of danger when you were right in the thick of it with no escape.

A shadow descended over her face like a light being quenched. "You do, don't you?"

"Think less of Lukasz? I know if you loved him, he must've been a good guy. I mean, he could have avoided going into service at all."

"I know it's probably hard for you to understand. After all, you were on the front lines and fought with courage."

"I don't know I'd say courage so much as I had a kind of foolish notion I was saving the world. Being a hero. But I seen a lot of things, done a lot of things I won't ever forget—can't forget. The way I was brought up though, that's what you did. When your country calls, you answer. But it sounds like Lukasz helped out the best way he could. Our medics were some of the bravest guys I knew, rushing in under fire to drag injured men to safety."

I could tell she didn't know whether to believe me or not, and I was still trying to sort it out in my own head, though I was inclined to think it was okay with me. After all, my pal Joey Flanagan spent the war at a desk job in Washington, D.C. where the biggest threat he'd faced was paper cuts from all the filing he did. What Jankowski had done, helping the wounded and dying in the theater of war was a heckuva lot more dangerous, and he'd paid the ultimate price for his service.

Which brought me back to the question of the photo. "But if Lukasz went down with his ship, how do you think this photo ended up back here on dry land?"

"I don't know, unless he left it behind on shore before they sailed. How did you come by it? Is it something to do with the woman at the theater?"

"I think so. Maudie and I found out where the other victim, the unconscious guy, was staying. When we searched his room, we found this. And what's more, I swung by the morgue and the dead woman had a second photo similar to this one in her purse."

"Setting aside the fact you've been treading a fine line with interfering in a police investigation—"

"Now don't you start. Flanagan's already been lecturing me. If he'd been more forthcoming with some inside dope, we wouldn't have had to stoop to such underhanded measures."

"That doesn't sound like him. You two are usually as thick as thieves."

"Yeah, I think he must have something on his mind. I'm wondering if there's some trouble on the home front he hasn't told me about. He seemed awful touchy when I joked about his wife today."

"This is an important case. The possible murder of a young woman. The mysterious circumstances of her death. The papers—your paper—will be full of it. Maybe he's just anxious to do everything by the book."

"That's what he said."

"So, are you telling me you stole this photo from the hotel room? Don't you think you crossed a line?"

"I didn't mean to. I kind of panicked when I saw it was you. Or might be you. And then it was too late to produce it, like, hey, Joey, I just happened to find this photo tucked inside my hat."

"You were trying to protect me? That's sweet, Jim, but I don't have anything to hide. We should take the photo down to the station and confess all. I don't know how, but maybe I can help their investigation. There must be some reason these people have a photograph of me and Lukasz."

"Do you think they could be relatives of his? Or friends?"

"Lukasz was an orphan, like me. That is, he knew who his parents were, but they both had died by the time he was sixteen. He never mentioned any but the most distant relatives of his parents back in Poland to me. People he knew about but wasn't in touch with. I suppose it's possible he contacted some of them while his ship was docked. Maybe they'd fled to England or moved there at some point, and he met up with them and showed them the pictures, but I don't think he would have left the photos behind on purpose. He told me he was going to keep them with him always as a lucky charm."

She suddenly jumped up and ran to the oven, heaving a sigh of relief when she opened the door, pulling out the tray of cookies. "Just caught them before they burned. You can taste test them for me while I change my clothes so we can go into town to talk to the police."

"I wouldn't bother changing, if I was you," I replied, pointing at the window in the kitchen door. Flanagan's big Irish face was peering in at us, and he didn't look happy. "I think the long arm of the law's caught up with me."

CHAPTER ELEVEN

*V*ictoria crossed the kitchen and opened the door. "Detective Flanagan, what good timing. We were about to pay you a visit."

"You'll pardon my saying that don't seem a likely story, Mrs. J." He glared at me. "Haven't been able to get this goon out of my hair all day. Then when I want him, he's nowhere to be found."

"Whataya mean, Joey? Here I am, large as life. And I know you ain't calling Victoria a liar," I added, getting to my feet, always ready to rumble with anyone who dared cast aspersions on the love of my life.

Joey came up into my face. "That's as may be, but who do you suppose was asking me about the big 'detective' with the scar who'd paid him a visit in the morgue?"

"So? I might have happened by there. I'm a reporter. I go all kinda places. Investigating, you know. Maybe you should try it sometime."

Joey huffed and I puffed. It was Victoria who stepped in between us with a plate of hot cookies that smelled like heaven and a sharp word for both of us. "You two Neanderthals need to settle down. Sit, and I'll make us some coffee. Now," she added in a voice that meant business when she saw we were gonna be stubborn about it.

I was first to back down, being respectful of my future wife's feelings in the matter. I sat and grabbed a cookie, devouring it in two seconds flat.

Joey couldn't hide a smirk. "You got chocolate smeared all over your chin. What are you? A five-year-old?"

"No, but I know somebody who's been acting like one. What's up with you anyway?"

"I'm trying to run a murder investigation here, but every which way I turn, you're one step ahead of me. Falling over suspects at the theater, breaking into hotel rooms, and now I find you've been sticking your nose in at the morgue. You're pushing it, Jimmy. Just 'cause we go way back, don't make you immune to consequences. Interfering with police business is against the law."

"You're only sore because I helped solve the last couple of big cases for you guys—"

"You can stop right there. Almost getting yourself killed in the first case and turning over a murderer to a couple of vigilantes in the other hardly counts as being helpful. I guess you think it's funny I almost got fired and lost my pension because of you?"

"I thought you smoothed all that over with your boss."

"I did—just. But it took some doing, and I had to promise him no more meddling from my old pal. He's watching me like a hawk now. If word gets back to him what you been up to today, I'm right back in the soup. So I mean it, Jimmy. Type up your pretty words for the paper and leave the investigating to us."

"I wouldn't do nothing on purpose to hurt you and Doreen, Joey. You know that. But I got a job to do too. I'm the one who'll be fired if I don't keep Morty supplied with the goods."

"Am I supposed to weep for you when you got a cushy set up here to fall back on? And a dame with loads of moolah lying around to keep you in the style you've become accustomed to."

That did it. I stood up swinging. Joey blocked the worst of my right to his jaw but missed the left to his solar plexus that knocked the wind out of him. I would have followed it up with a fist to the nose if I hadn't had a gallon or two of cold dishwater dumped over my head all unexpected.

"That's enough! If you can't behave like two adults, then leave this house."

Victoria's eyes were blazing, and I can't say I blamed her. I was abashed I'd let my temper get the better of me, but he'd touched on a sore spot with that crack about being a kept man. He knew I was sensitive about the fact Victoria had so much more money than me. It was his fault for pushing me, but I shoulda been the bigger man.

I reached for a dish towel to wipe the worst of the wet away and sat back down while Joey recovered enough breath to mutter an apology to Victoria.

"Accepted. I know Jim sometimes skirts the line when he's reporting, but you must agree with me that he means well and is pursuing the same end as the police, which is to discover the truth. You two should be working together, not fighting. To start with, Jim, why don't you show Detective Flanagan the photograph."

"What photograph?" Joey asked, bristling again.

I produced the snap, knowing he wasn't gonna like it when I explained how I came by it, and he didn't.

"You stole this from a suspect's hotel room? A room you had no business being in at all, I might add. Any judge in the district would throw the book at you for this."

"I know, Joey. It ain't like I make a habit of it. I was rattled when I saw it and then you guys was there and well, I ain't too proud to admit when I made a mistake, but if you look close, maybe you'll understand why."

Flanagan examined the photo. "Doc at the morgue found one like this on the dead woman but it wasn't this clear." He looked up at Victoria. "Woman looks like your twin sister. Is it? Or is it you?"

"It's definitely me and my husband, Lukasz Jankowski. Or husband-to-be at the time of the photograph to be precise. There was a strip of four from a photo booth. He had two and I have the other two. This is one of the ones Lukasz took away with him to war. How it ended up back here with a strange man, I have no idea."

"How can you be sure he's a stranger? You ain't seen him."

"That's true. Maybe I should come with you to talk to him. If he was a friend or relative of Lukasz's, it might explain why he has the photograph."

"It's an idea. You say you have the other two. Are you absolutely sure this ain't one of the ones you hung on to?"

"Yes. We looked at those photos so many times together, I had all the poses memorized, but I can fetch the other two from upstairs if you like?"

Flanagan indicated he did like. When she'd left the room, he turned to me. "For all I give you a hard time about it, Victoria's a swell lady so I didn't wanna suggest it in front of her, but what's to stop this mug in the hospital from being Lukasz back from the war and shacking up with another woman?"

"Only the fact her husband's swimming with the fishes at the bottom of the Atlantic."

"How sure are we of that, though? Maybe he deserted Victoria or the Navy or both. Wouldn't be the first guy to use the chaos of war to make a break with his past."

"She got an official telegram from the War Office. Showed it to me once. How often do they make that kind of mistake?"

"More often than you might think. Don't forget, I was pushing papers during the war. We saw things. ID and notifications weren't always one hundred percent correct. The brass did the best they could, but when a ship goes down, taking the bodies with it, what they did was account for all the survivors and list the rest of the crew as missing and presumed dead."

"If the guy at the hospital is Victoria's husband and was trying to ditch her and start a new life, maybe with the woman at the theater, then why come back here at all? Why run the risk?"

"What risk? With his face all burned, do you think even his wife would recognize him right off?"

"Only if he had some distinguishing feature or by his voice maybe," I suggested.

"This guy's voice is all messed up. Probably from whatever did the dirty to his face. It's so scratchy and hoarse, it's all you can do to make out what he's saying, when he's not speaking in foreign mumbo-jumbo, that is."

"So, you're saying Lukasz was among the survivors but wasn't counted for some reason. Maybe he got burned in the explosion from the torpedoes. Lost his dog tags. They couldn't identify him. Shipped to a military hospital as unknown and then, what? Pretended he'd lost his memory? Skipped out of the hospital before he could be ID'd?"

"Maybe. That's one scenario. But think about this, how do we even know Jankowski was on that ship when it sunk?"

"Because he would have come back to me and Karolina if he wasn't."

CHAPTER TWELVE

*V*ictoria had snuck back up on us while we was talking. She handed the photos over to Flanagan and sat down across from me. Guess she didn't want to get too close, as I was still dripping from the earlier dishwater incident, but she reached over the table and took one of my hands. I gave hers a squeeze that was half apology, half attempt at comfort.

"I'm sorry you overheard us, Mrs. J, but we gotta consider all the angles."

"I understand, Detective Flanagan, and I understand you can't just take my word for it, but I know in my heart, if he had survived, he would have found his way home. He knew I was with child and was as excited as I was. He was not a duplicitous man or in any way a sneak. He wore his heart on his sleeve for all to see. The actions you are imagining would have been unthinkable for him. He was proud to be doing his part in the war and would never have voluntarily deserted either our country or me in our time of need."

Flanagan looked redder in the face than usual but stood his ground. "If I had a century note for every wife—or husband, for that matter—who thought they knew their spouse through and through only to wind up disappointed, I could retire right now. As far as I'm concerned, anybody is capable of deceit in the right circumstances, even someone you think loves you more than anyone else in the world."

There was a lot of bitterness in his statement that brought up the question in my mind again about his own marriage. I made a note to drop by his place and check in with Doreen. See if something was up with them two. I'd always thought they were the perfect Irish love-birds, billing and cooing in a way that would've made you sick if it wasn't so sincere. I hated to think there was trouble in paradise.

As a man about to embark on the journey of matrimony myself, I preferred to think it would be all smooth sailing, but I guess any two people can hit a rocky patch now and again. I hoped Victoria and I would be the exception, but we each had a mind of our own. There was bound to be times we wouldn't see eye to eye on something.

Victoria seemed to sense there was personal feeling behind Flanagan's observation, as her face and voice softened when she replied.

"It's true we can't know everything about another person. No one has had a more painful lesson in that than me. My own mother was far from the woman I thought she was for years. But there's an easy way to settle this. I'll come to the hospital and look at this man. He won't have changed so much that I wouldn't recognize him."

"He might be more changed than you think. Maybe Jimmy didn't mention it, but his face ain't in great shape. Old burn wounds. Consistent with some kind of injury caused by, oh, I don't know, getting in the way of a torpedo explosion maybe."

"How horrible for him, however the wounds were inflicted, but I will know whether or not it is Lukasz. I have no doubt of that."

"Well, can't hurt none for you to have a look at him, and it might help us out. I'll hang on to these photos for now until we figure out what the connection is."

Victoria didn't look so happy at that. I couldn't blame her. She didn't have many souvenirs from the short time she and Lukasz had together, and I was wearing one of them in the form of her hubby's best hat. But she just nodded and made short work of running back upstairs to change into an outfit she considered good enough to be seen in town while I headed out to the cottage and changed into a dry suit.

Following Flanagan's sedan in Victoria's red Caddy, neither of us talked much. She looked relaxed at the wheel, driving with her usual confidence. She was sure the man at the hospital wasn't Lukasz, but I couldn't help wonder what it would mean for us if she was wrong. They'd had such a special connection that she hadn't even looked at another man until she met me. Don't ask me what she saw in my mangled kisser that attracted her. Whatever it was, I was afraid it wasn't enough to compete with her first love if he was to reappear in the flesh, even if his face now wasn't any improvement on mine.

We pulled into a couple of empty spaces across from the hospital but didn't make it inside. Fink and Wilson were standing around on the sidewalk out front looking even more confused than was usual for those two dim bulbs. Fink caught sight of Flanagan bearing down on them and gave Wilson a warning tap on the arm.

"Hey, there, Boss," Wilson said.

"Don't 'Boss' me! What are you knuckleheads doing down here? You're supposed to be guarding the suspect until your relief shows up."

The two cops exchanged looks as if they was each waiting for the other to speak up. Fink broke first.

"You see, Boss, it's like this…"

I had a sudden premonition. "Don't tell us you lost the guy."

Flanagan snorted. "How could they lose a sick guy handcuffed to a hospital bed? Right?"

He turned a gimlet eye on the hapless pair, who had both swiped their hats down from their heads, kneading them nervously in their hands like they was gonna tear them to pieces.

"It ain't our fault," spluttered Fink.

Flanagan exploded and let out a string of syllables I won't sully your delicate ears with.

"Uh, Boss, there's a lady present," ventured Wilson, indicating Victoria. She was standing by trying not to look amused at this gambit to stem the invective raining down on their heads.

Joey took a deep breath and pressed his meaty lips together with an expression like he was attempting to swallow back bile. "Okay, maybe you two can explain to us how a guy who's barely conscious and chained to a bed is now missing."

"He woke up about a half hour ago," said Fink. "Said he was feeling better. Wanted to get up and stretch his legs. Didn't seem no harm in it. He acted weak as a kitten. But once we got to the end of the hallway, he took off like a bat out of hell for the stairs."

"Yeah, Boss," added Wilson. "He sprinted faster than one of those Olympic runners. I think he might've been faking how sick he was."

"You think so, Einstein?" Flanagan spit. "And neither one of you two could keep up with him?"

"We was gaining on him when an orderly got in between us with a pregnant lady on a gurney. She was hollering and grabbing onto anything she could reach, and we got all tangled up and, well…"

"Yeah, I get the picture. That's some fine police work right there. You two are gonna be nominated for medals if you keep it up. Did you at least call it in so everyone would be on the lookout for him?"

They exchanged looks.

"Jeez, I gotta do everything myself. You and Mrs. J might as well scram," Joey said to me. "Who knows when we'll catch up with this guy with the head start he got."

"Kinda suspicious him taking it on the lam, ain't it?" I observed.

"Yeah, not what you'd expect from an innocent bystander. All the more reason to track him down. We'll be in touch if we get hold of him again."

Flanagan and the comedy team of Fink and Wilson jumped in Joey's car. I could hear him barking orders into the police radio as he revved the engine. Wasn't long before they sped off leaving me and Victoria alone.

"Shall I drive you back home, or do you want to stop by the paper?" she said.

"Neither. I'm inclined to do a little more investigating. Want to come along?"

"I thought you'd never ask."

CHAPTER THIRTEEN

We waited until Joey and his boys were out of sight, then entered the hospital. I guided Victoria upstairs to where they'd been guarding the guy. We were in luck. Looked like no one had bothered to start cleaning and setting the room to rights. Guess they hadn't gotten word yet their patient was AWOL.

"Let's take a look around," I said. "It's a longshot, but you never know. We might find something. Those clowns didn't even think to come back up here and search for any clues after they lost him."

We poked around. It wasn't a big space, so it didn't take long. Other than the guy's clothes in the closet there wasn't much to see. I checked all the pockets and even stripped the sheets off the bed but found nothing. I saw Victoria looking at a pad and pencil left on the bedside table.

"Anything written on it?"

"Looks like the top sheet was torn off, but let's try something I saw in the movies once," she said, taking the pencil and moving the edge of the lead lightly back and forth across the paper. "Ta da!"

She handed me the pad. The pencil had brought out the impression of the handwriting from the missing page.

"That's a neat trick! Looks like an address. 805 Fleming Ave."

"Not just any address," she replied, looking troubled. "Don't you recognize it? That's Mr. Klein's haberdashery shop."

"Hey, I think you're right."

"I know I'm right. I've been there often enough in my life. His daughter Esther was one of my best friends growing up," she reminded me. "She was the only friend I had outside of the Sisters of Mercy until I met Lukasz."

"Huh. A weird kind of coincidence, ain't it? First we find these photos of you and Lukasz and now, this address for the hatmaker of this very hat you gifted me and was made special for your husband," I said, touching the brim of that selfsame topper.

"It is strange. I suppose this missing man could be in the market for a new hat, but someone on the run from the police isn't going to wait around to have one specially made. He'd just walk into any department store and buy one."

"Yeah, although he left his clothes here in the closet, so he's running around in a hospital gown. Should make him pretty conspicuous."

"We ought to let Detective Flanagan know about this right away, Jim."

"I guess. Although, it was their fault for not coming back up here to investigate. I feel like we're doing their work for them. Might as well go all the way. What say we run over to Klein's real quick and see if the guy's made an appearance? If he has, I can detain him while you call the police. They wanted you to talk to him anyway. This might be your chance."

She gave me a look that made me regret for half a second I didn't have Maudie with me instead of Victoria. Maudie would have been out the door in a flash, but she was no substitute for my Victoria in any other way. Besides, deep down, I knew it was the right thing to do. We found a telephone down the hall at the nurses' station, and I made my report to Joey. He didn't sound thrilled at my further interference but had to admit it was useful info.

"They're headed over there," I reported.

"Good. So are we."

"We are? But what about police interference?"

"Like you said, they wanted to see if I could identify the man. Besides, it's been too long since I've visited with Mr. Klein. I'd love to have an update on how Esther is doing. We lost touch after she got married and had her kids. Maybe I'll even buy myself a new hat. We do have a special day coming up, after all," Victoria added, sliding her hand around the crook of my arm.

I enjoyed the feel of it there but wondered about our special day. I'd always felt a guy like me didn't have the kind of luck it took to land someone like Victoria as a wife. There was a part of me kept expecting to wake up from the dream, and I didn't appreciate the way events kept circling back to things she and Lukasz had done together.

What if—just, what if—this was Lukasz returned from the dead? Victoria's conviction he wouldn't have abandoned her was touching, but I'd seen how war can change a man. It changed me. Who's to say it hadn't done something to Lukasz too? Turned him into someone as unrecognizable on the inside as he was on the outside. There was no doubt the guy we were hunting had been through something bad. Those burns were proof of that. Enough to turn anyone sour. Maybe even make them into a killer.

But what I couldn't figure was, if it was Lukasz, what was in it for him turning back up here? Even all these years later, he could be in big trouble with the Navy for desertion. It would've been safer to stay overseas the way other deserters had after the war. Wanting to be reunited with his wife was certainly a motivation, but as far as we could tell, he'd made no effort to contact Victoria yet. And what about this other woman? How did she fit into the picture?

The whole thing gave me an uneasy feeling. The wedding was only a week and a half away, but a lot can happen in that amount of time was the thought in my head as Victoria pulled up in front of old man Klein's shop.

We walked in to be greeted by Mitzi Leonard, who had a brother who was quite fond of Q's sister, so we were all old pals.

"How are you, Mr. Malhaven? And Mrs. Jankowski, how nice to see you. I heard from Sam the two of you are getting married soon.

Have you come for a bridal hat? They're all the rage this year with such darling little veils. We've sold a lot of them to other June brides."

"Yes, I think I will order one if you think Mr. Klein has time to make it. Our wedding is on the sixteenth."

"Usually, we'd require more lead time, but I'm sure he'd make an exception. He thinks so highly of you, you know."

"How kind. Is he here?"

"Not at the moment. He and one of his assistants went over to the garment district to pick out some more trim and ornaments. We've been so busy lately that he was running out."

"What a shame we've missed him. I was going to inquire after Esther. I haven't seen her in ages."

"You know she and her husband have had a terrible time. Their youngest got polio. She's in one of those iron lungs at the hospital. They don't know when or if she'll ever recover from it."

"Oh, no! How dreadful. I hadn't heard."

"It only happened a week ago. Mr. Klein was so downhearted. He dotes on all his grandchildren, but little Alice is his favorite, though he wouldn't ever admit it. She used to come in the store all the time and play at making hats with him. She's only six, poor lamb."

I could tell Victoria was broke up at hearing that. She had a soft spot for kids. I hadn't thought much about them myself until we'd taken care of Lily back in the spring. I couldn't imagine a young child trapped in one of those machines day after day. That was no life for anybody, but I'd seen on the newsreel a lot of them recovered enough to breathe on their own. Maybe Klein's granddaughter would be one of the lucky ones.

"That's a tough break," I said. "You'll have to give Mr. Klein and family our sympathies."

"And tell him I'll stop by the hospital and visit," Victoria added.

"Esther will appreciate that. She talks about you all the time and the fun you used to have when you were girls. Not that you're so old now," Mitzi added, turning red.

Victoria laughed. "No offense taken. It's true it's been many years since we used to run around together. I'm sorry I've not done more to keep in touch. I'll try to make it up to her now. Maybe there's something I can do to help."

"The treatment is terribly expensive. They want to send her to that Warm Springs place—you know, where FDR used to go—if she gets well enough to travel. Mr. Klein is helping them out as much as he can. They're probably too proud to accept help from anyone outside the family, but maybe they would for Alice's sake."

"I'll offer anyway."

"You are nice, just like Esther and Mr. Klein always say. Shall I tell him you came by? You can pick a hat from our design book or ask him to make something special for you."

"That's not the only reason we came by," I interrupted. "There's a man who may come looking for Mr. Klein. Easy to recognize 'cause his face is scarred even worse than mine."

As I said it, we all heard the bell above the front door chime and turned to look. You guessed it. As I always say, speak of the Devil and he shall appear.

CHAPTER FOURTEEN

It was the guy from the movie theater alright, unless there was more than one mook with a toasted face wandering around town. He looked like he'd picked through somebody's laundry that was hanging out to dry, as he was dressed in a mismatch of clothes, none of which fit exactly right. His feet were bare and black from the grime of the city streets.

He looked at my scarred face with a kind of grimace, like he was acknowledging a fellow sufferer. I thought he was gonna come in and chat, but his eyes shifted to my right and landed on Victoria. The burns didn't allow him the greatest variety in facial expression, but the way he turned tail and ran made me think he recognized her and wasn't interested in palavering just then.

I sprinted after him as best I could on my two busted-up legs. He was shorter than me, so I had the advantage in stride, but he was definitely more nimble. Whatever had caused the burns on his face hadn't affected his athleticism. I kept at it though, concentrating so hard on not falling, I almost didn't notice the blur that passed me on the sidewalk.

It was Victoria, running like a gazelle in her bare feet. She must've kicked off her heels to get better traction. Some guys might feel shown up, but I was just filled with admiration at her speed. She was always full of surprises.

The guy never once looked back to see if we were gaining on him, knocking over trash cans and anything else he could lay his hands on to try and trip us up. He caught a break when he got a couple of blocks away from Klein's and saw a bus about to pull away from the curb. He banged on the door and jumped aboard as the bus roared away from us.

I caught up to Victoria and put an arm around her, more for my support than hers. The old wounds in my legs were on fire, and I was puffing like a freight train.

Victoria looked up at me with concern in her eyes. "You all right, sweetheart?"

"I think so. I didn't know you could run like that."

She grinned. "I was on the girl's track team at Sisters of Mercy. Won some trophies. I think I still have them around somewhere. But I was always wearing shoes before. These city streets are hard on the feet. My stockings are ruined."

I swung her up in my arms. My legs might be shot, but I had plenty of gusto in the upper body. She protested, but I carried her back to Klein's shop to save her delicate soles any more wear and tear.

There was a welcoming committee waiting for us. Klein was back. Flanagan had shown up too. I wasn't looking forward to explaining how we had literally chased away their prime suspect, but Joey just shook his head.

"You see before you a defeated man, Jimmy. I don't know what I ever done to you. Thought we were pals, but pals don't do each other this way. Miss Leonard here was explaining what happened. Seeing as you're back empty-handed except for Mrs. J there, I can only assume your chase was a bust, so now we're back to square one again. I could yell at you some more, but I give up. I'm tired, and nothing gets through that thick skull of yours."

"Detective Flanagan, I really must take responsibility this time," said Victoria as I lowered her to the floor. She stepped back into her shoes. "It was my idea to meet you here. I naturally feel an interest in the case and thought I might be able to speak to the man. I hope you will accept my apologies. It does seem seeing me startled him into taking off again, but surely that only reinforces my right to know what's going on."

"I ain't gonna argue with you neither, Mrs. J. I will observe there is a proper procedure that oughta be followed. The police catch the bad guys and bring them in at which point any pertinent witnesses get their chance. That's the way it works most places, but here I got a whole army of private eyes thinking they can do better than we can."

I had to object. "It wasn't us let the guy slip out from right under our noses at the hospital."

"You don't gotta rub it in. I've given Fink and Wilson twenty-four hours to track him down or they're both going on report. And we've got every other available cop on the beat keeping their eyes peeled. This city ain't that big. He won't be able to hide for long, not with his face. I've spoken to Mr. Klein here. He's got no more idea than you do why this guy wanted to pay him a visit, so I'm heading back to the station. I'll be sitting by the phone eagerly waiting for you to give me my next big break."

And with that bitter observation, Flanagan left, banging the front door so hard, the bell over it was knocked off and fell to the ground with a sour clang.

Klein picked it up, looking at it ruefully. "I don't think the detective was too pleased, was he?"

"It really is my fault," said Victoria. "I encouraged Jim to come here to see if we could meet with the man. And I wanted to see you, of course."

Klein patted her fondly on the arm. "You know you are always most welcome, my dear. Mitzi says you would like for me to make you a hat for your wedding just as I did for Lukasz for your first one. I see you have managed not to put any more holes in it, Mr. Malhaven."

When Victoria had gifted me with her late husband's hat, I'd promised to take good care of it, but Mr. Klein had already repaired it twice, for bullet holes of all things. I could only hope that old saw about bad things coming in threes was just a saying. My luck couldn't hold out forever.

"I am very happy for you both," continued Klein. "Lukasz was a good man, but none of us can grieve forever. Life is for the living. I have long wished for Victoria to find another worthy of her affections and now she has."

I had to blush. "That's a big compliment coming from you, sir. I appreciate it. Guess Flanagan filled you in a bit on why we're so interested in this missing guy. Sounds as if you don't have any idea why he might have wanted to see you."

"Not a clue, as I believe they would say in these detective novels that are so popular."

"Did Detective Flanagan mention this man had a photograph of me and Lukasz from before we were married?" asked Victoria.

"No. How strange. A relative or a friend, perhaps?"

"Possibly, but then why did he take off when he saw me? And why not come seek me out when he first came to town. It sounds like he's been here a few days at least."

"It is a puzzle, but one I will leave in the hands of those far more capable than me to solve. My talent is hats, and I have in mind quite a special one for you, Victoria. Mitzi, my sketchbook, please."

Mitzi pulled an oversized, leather-bound book out from under the sales counter. Klein opened it to a blank page and made quick work of sketching out a topper that more than met with Victoria's approval.

"That's perfect," she said. "We're to be married at the City Courthouse on the sixteenth at 2 pm. We wanted to keep it quite informal and quiet given everything we've been through, but I would love for you and Mrs. Klein, and you and Sam too, Mitzi, if you like, to come by. There will be a small reception back out at Wynter's Hill afterward. And Esther and her husband, of course, although I understand from Mitzi they may be too preoccupied right now for such an event. I'm so sorry to hear about young Alice."

Tears rose to the old man's eyes at the mention of his granddaughter. "Such a light she is. I should go to the hospital more often, but to see her like that—it is more than I can bear."

"I'll go by and visit if you think it might lift Esther's spirits."

"That would be a good thing, my dear. She has missed your friendship, but it is often the way that old friends drift apart."

"I should never have allowed it," said Victoria. "I'll try and make it up to her."

We parted, with Klein promising to have the hat done in plenty of time and also to let us know if the missing link showed at his store again. Victoria dropped me at the paper with plans to pick me up after she checked in at the hospital with Esther.

I hopped it to my desk and pounded out a story on my trusty Underwood with the exciting events of the day. Did I forget to add the detail of the photos? Well, yes, but to be fair, I figured Flanagan might want to keep it close to his vest for now as we still didn't know the connection with Victoria and Lukasz. I'd already seen the love of my life dragged through the tabloids when it turned out her mother was a gun-toting drug kingpin. I wasn't gonna mention the photo unless or until I had to.

If Morty found out, he'd rake me over the coals and probably assign the story to another reporter who didn't have a stake in it. That was the last thing I wanted. I needed to stay close to the action so I could protect Victoria as much as possible. Not that she would ever ask me to. In fact, she'd probably get pretty mad at the idea, but sometimes what you don't know, can't hurt you. Right?

CHAPTER FIFTEEN

*V*ictoria was late picking me up. She and her old pal Esther had got to catching up at the hospital and lost track of the clock, but I didn't mind. I passed the time filling Q in on the developments since we'd parted ways at the hospital morgue. He had updates for me as well.

"My uncle telephoned. He'll deny ever telling us this, but the autopsy on the woman showed she died of a heart attack."

"A heart attack, huh? Seems fishy for a young woman like that. At least, she looked young."

"The doctor estimated mid to late twenties."

"Evidence of heart trouble?"

"Not that he could find nor other obvious signs of disease. They're going to test for common poisons next, but the results will take a while. And that's not all."

"Do tell, Q."

"She showed signs of having given birth not long ago. Weeks to a few months."

"Interesting. If she had a baby, where is it now?"

"Maybe it didn't survive, or she gave it up for adoption? Left it with relatives or friends while she traveled?"

"Yeah, lots of possibilities there. We still don't know for sure what the connection is between her and the burn guy, but if they was hitched, maybe they had a baby together too."

"That is just conjecture, Mr. Malhaven. There may have been no connection between them at all. You said the clerk at the hotel was sure no one had been staying with the man or visited him before you and Miss Adams."

"It's asking a little much to think we found the guy unconscious at the same movie house as the dead woman, and that those are two totally unrelated events. And don't forget, the guy had a photo of Victoria and Lukasz in his hotel room, and the woman had one in her purse. That ain't a coincidence."

"True. Didn't they also find a suitcase with the woman?"

"Yeah, and a train ticket from New York to Chicago in her purse. They found a train ticket on the guy too, but I don't think they were travelling together. He'd been here five days the clerk said, and the woman looked as if she was just getting into town when they met up. I'm thinking it was inconvenient somehow her showing up. He might not have been too happy to be reunited. Maybe he had to do something quick to get rid of her."

"Are you saying he went to meet her with a plan for murder?" Q asked.

"That, or he did some mighty quick thinking on his feet, but most of us don't have poison just sitting around in case we have a brainstorm to off someone. Although now I think about it, he did have a whole pharmacy in his hotel room, and they said at the hospital they thought he'd OD'd on something. Maybe he offered to share some drugs with the girl, took some himself to show it was harmless but miscalculated, and before he could make his escape, he's passed out on the stairs."

"It is likely with those severe burn wounds that he took narcotics for pain. The toxicology report should show if she had anything in her system."

"It could be a cagey way to murder someone. Let's face it, if he'd managed to get away from the theater, the cops would probably never have made a connection between him and this girl. Not unless they manage to ID her, and it traces back to him. But they got no idea who he is either. He could have melted away with no one the wiser."

"But would he have left? He must have come to town for a reason. We don't get a lot of casual tourists here in Carsworth City, do we?"

"That's for sure," I agreed. "Who would come here unless they knew somebody already? The photo bothers me. And you should've seen how quick he turned tail and ran when he caught sight of Victoria at Klein's."

"Maybe he didn't like my face."

I turned around at that low voice I knew so well. "As if. Anybody who don't like your face has got mush for brains."

Victoria laughed. "Thank you, sweetheart. I see you and Mr. Sutherland are discussing our mystery man. Any bright ideas?"

"Just hashing it out a bit. Turns out the woman at the theater died of a heart attack. No obvious cause. She'd given birth not so long ago too."

That turned the smile off her face. "A baby? I hope it's all right. There's been no mention of a child being found has there?"

"No, but I wouldn't worry. Could be a thousand explanations for that."

She didn't look convinced.

Q decided to change the subject. "Have you written your story already, Mr. Malhaven? You still have time to update it with the autopsy information on the woman."

"I think I'll leave that info until tomorrow's editions. Don't want to get your uncle in Dutch with the doc if he figures out where we got the intel so quick. Maybe I can pry it out of Flanagan if he's cooled down. It ain't like him to be this stingy with the insider dope. We can hope he was just having a bad day. I'll see you tomorrow, Q."

"Good night, Mr. Malhaven. Mrs. Jankowski. I hope you have a most pleasant evening."

We returned the sentiment and headed home. Victoria filled me in on her visit with Esther.

"It was wonderful to see her. Almost like old times, but oh, Jim, it would break your heart to see that little girl in that awful iron lung. I mean, it is keeping her alive, so Esther is grateful, but for a child to be trapped like that for who knows how long."

"I heard a lot of them get better though after a few weeks. That they can wean them off those machines."

"Many do, but not all. I hope she'll be one of the lucky ones. She was so sweet about it too. Children that young normally aren't so patient. I promised Esther I would drop by every day and give her and her husband a rest. Mrs. Klein and Esther's mother-in-law have been taking turns looking after their other children so they can spend more time at the hospital, but it has to take a toll."

"Did you know her hubby before they got married?"

"Daniel? He's how I met Lukasz. They were best friends, and Daniel was Esther's boyfriend when I first ran into her, which is how I met her. Bowled her right over on the sidewalk because I wasn't paying attention to where I was going, but she was so nice about it. We started talking and that was that." Victoria smiled at the memory. "Esther invited me out to a movie one Saturday afternoon with her and Daniel. Lukasz tagged along and the rest, as they say, is history. Daniel was Lukasz's best man, and Esther was my maid of honor. It's a shame I let our friendship lapse, but I must admit, I found it harder to be around the two of them after Lukasz and Karolina died. It was difficult to see them together and so happy with their babies when I had nothing left."

"Understandable."

"But not terribly nice of me. I haven't had so many friends in my life that I should be careless with the few I do have."

"It's never too late. Sounds like she don't hold it against you."

"No, Esther is just as wonderful as her father. The Kleins were always so kind to me. They are good people through and through."

"And Mr. Klein knows his way around a hat, don't he?"

"He learned from his father, who learned from his father before him. Three generations have worked in that same store. I hope many more generations will as well."

"No doubt," I said, little realizing just how short a future Klein's had in front of it.

CHAPTER SIXTEEN

I was jerked out of a sound sleep the next morning by a frantic rat-a-tat-tatting at the cottage door. I stumbled to open it, with my robe only halfway on, and found Victoria waiting for me. She was looking a bit more put together than me in a cute, patterned dress, her hair pulled back in a high ponytail. If the frantic knocking hadn't already alerted me, the look on her face told me something was very, very wrong.

"Oh, Jim! Esther just called me. It's the store. Klein's. It's on fire!"

"What? Is everybody okay?" I knew old man Klein and his wife lived in rooms over top the store and braced myself for the worst.

"They got out in time, but the store may be past saving. I'm going to drive over there to see what's happening, and if there's anything I can do for them. I thought you might want to come along."

"You betcha. It'll be a big story for the paper."

She made a face at me. "It's not just a headline. These are our friends."

"I know, honey. That came out wrong, but I'm still half asleep. Gimme a minute."

I splashed cold water all over my face, feeling the bristles on my chin but not wanting to waste time shaving. The world would have to take me as is. Shrugged into a suit, and we were on the road again. It was barely light yet but light enough for us to make out the smoke in the distance over downtown. Must have been a big blaze to kick up that kind of soot and ash.

By the time we got there, it looked as if every citizen in the city had crowded into the narrow streets around Klein's. We had to park far away and push our way through to get to the front of the line. We found his wife and daughter drowning in tears, but Klein was just standing, ashen-faced, as he watched his lifelong business and home smoldering down to a shambles.

The fire brigade was dousing the place with their hoses full force, but it was obvious it was a lost cause. Their goal now was just to keep the fire from re-igniting and spreading to the neighboring buildings. The second story had collapsed onto the first, and the street was littered with bricks fallen from the ruined façade. Klein's as we knew it was no more.

Victoria embraced the women and led them away from the heat and chaos. I stood with Mr. Klein, laying a sympathetic hand on his shoulder. He looked as if he'd aged a thousand years since we last saw him.

"That's it, Mr. Malhaven. Klein's Haberdashery. Founded 1873. Destroyed 1951. I suppose seventy-eight years is a fair run for any business."

"Don't talk like that, Mr. Klein. You can rebuild and be back at it in no time. You got fire insurance, don't you?"

"Yes, but I am getting to be an old man. To start again at my age." He shook his head at the thought. "What have I done to deserve this misfortune?"

"Things could be worse. You and the missus made it out okay."

"That is true. It was fortunate I was up so early. I wanted to work on Victoria's bridal hat. Make it something extra special for her. When I got to the top of the stairs that go down to the store, I smelled the smoke. I woke up my wife, and we were able to make it out the fire escape before the smoke got bad, but it was too late by the time the firemen arrived. So many finished commissions ruined. So many people who were depending on me."

"Look, you know you won't find a bigger fan of wearing a topper than me, but at the end of the day, a hat is only a hat. It's more important you and the wife made it out safe. The rest is fixable, like this fedora of mine, but people ain't so easily repaired."

"I know you are right. I should be a grateful man, but it is hard to see my life's work reduced to rubble."

"It's a blow, any way you slice it. Any idea what sparked it?"

"I might be able to help with that." Flanagan was looming up behind us. He hadn't had a chance to shave either and looked as if he'd slept in his suit.

"Been talking to the Fire Captain. Can't say for sure, but there's a strong smell of gasoline all around the front door—well, at least where the front door used to be—and some half-burned rags."

Klein looked even more shocked at this news. "You are not saying someone deliberately set fire to my shop, Detective. Why would anyone do such a thing?"

"I was hoping you could tell me, Mr. Klein. Had any threats lately? Anything unusual happen?"

I had to break in at that question. "The guy you been chasing around showing up here was kinda unusual. Maybe he came back again, but I know you would've had some officers keeping an eye on the place just in case, right?"

Flanagan flushed red. "Fink and Wilson told me they had it covered."

"There you go. What'd they see?"

"Nothing but the inside of their eyelids. They admitted they both drifted off after midnight and didn't wake up until the sound of the fire engine siren entered their useless melons."

"Why haven't you thrown those palookas off this case? They gotta be two of the most incompetent mugs on the force."

"It ain't so easy. Fink's the boss's son-in-law."

"And Wilson?"

"His son."

"Jeez, that's a tough spot for you, but he can't blame you for this mess."

"Who d'you think he'd rather blame? The detective who let a murdering Nazi slip through his fingers last spring or his family? I know I'm the one that's gonna get it in the neck while those two nimrods will probably get a promotion."

"It is unfortunate they were not awake. They might have stopped the man, but again, what motive would he have to burn down my store?" asked Klein.

"I dunno, but he did write down your address at the hospital and showed up here yesterday. Maybe he has a grudge against you, or maybe he don't like Jews. There's more than a few of that type around."

"I am well aware, Detective Flanagan, but we've had no trouble in years. Not since the war."

"Just because we beat Hitler don't mean all the anti-Semites disappeared."

I had to object. "C'mon, Joey, you saying our mystery man traveled all the way to Carsworth City to burn down the shop of a random Jewish guy? Don't make sense. Besides, he came here yesterday like he was gonna visit. You don't think he planned to burn the store down in broad daylight. Maybe he just wanted a word with Mr. Klein."

"About what? A new hat?"

"Klein's daughter Esther and her husband were good friends of Lukasz and Victoria. This guy and the woman at the theater both had those photographs. There has to be some connection."

"So, he got scared away yesterday when he saw Victoria and decided to burn the place down instead. Where does that get him?" Joey asked.

"I don't know, but it's starting to seem like he had a plan that's unravelling. I don't think he planned for the woman at the theater, whether it was his wife or not, to show up here in town. He certainly didn't plan to get nabbed by the cops after passing out. He didn't plan on Victoria being there when he showed up at Klein's yesterday. I think what we got is someone who's not a genius at thinking on his feet and is digging himself deeper and deeper into a hole instead of getting closer to his goal."

"Which is?"

"How should I know? I ain't clairvoyant. We need to find the guy and ask him!"

"We? We who?"

"You and me. These mokes you got working for you are useless, and I don't wanna see you go under. Don't you think we'd get farther teaming up and sharing info? C'mon, Joey, whataya say," I added, sticking out one of my paws.

"Okay," he sighed deep and shook my hand. "But I have a feeling I'm gonna regret this."

CHAPTER SEVENTEEN

e started our partnership by sharing intel. I didn't have much new to add other than the extent of the connections between Klein's daughter and Victoria. He shared the autopsy results on the woman with me. I pretended to be shocked and amazed, not wanting to get Q's uncle into a jam.

The other big news he had was the contents of the woman's suitcase. A meager change of clothes and some toiletries, plain, average quality. Nothing special about them that would help identify where she might have come from. A much-creased letter written in a foreign language, and a pair of pink knitted baby booties.

"Baby booties, huh?" I said. "That's interesting. Doc says she'd given birth recently, but where's the baby?"

"Maybe it died," Joey suggested, "and the booties are like a souvenir, you know? Something to remember it by. Or her. Probably a girl since they're pink."

"What about the letter? Has it been translated?"

"Didn't get a chance yet. I have it here," he said, pulling it out of his suit pocket. "No one at the station recognized the language."

"Polish," said Mr. Klein. We'd gotten so caught up in our discussion, we'd forgotten about the poor guy standing there watching the ruin of a lifetime of work.

I think we must have both looked guilty as well as surprised because he smiled at us. "I have many Polish customers and have seen the language written down before."

"Can you read it?" Flanagan asked.

"Only a few words here and there, but I know someone who can. She is close by. I will take you there. Even though it is early, she is always up first thing."

"If she's like the rest of these gawkers, she's standing down here in the streets right now," I observed, gesturing to the crowd of excited onlookers. Not much happens in our city so there was a carnival atmosphere of barely respectful enjoyment on many of the faces.

"Not Mrs. Gomolka. She's 103 years old and no longer leaves her apartment as she can't manage the stairs. Her great granddaughter—or perhaps it is her great, great granddaughter, I forget—lives with her and takes care of her now. It isn't far," he added, leading the way through the crowd many of who, recognizing the victim of their current entertainment, gave way before him with downcast eyes. At least they had some shame left.

He led us over two blocks and around a corner to a small brick brownstone. Not far enough away we couldn't still smell the smoke, but at least there weren't any curious onlookers here. We walked up to the second floor. Klein knocked on the first door to the left at the top of the stairs. A sweet-faced girl of about sixteen answered with a look of curiosity on her face at the unexpected delegation.

"Good morning, Yvonne. So sorry to disturb you this early. These gentlemen thought Mrs. Gomolka might help translate a letter for them. I don't believe you know Polish, do you?"

"No, Mr. Klein. Ma tried to teach me but gave up in despair. I just don't have a talent for languages, but I'm sure Busia would be happy to do it. Please come in."

She ushered us into a cozy room with an electric fire turned up full blast despite it being summertime. A woman bent and crumpled like an old piece of tissue paper looked up at us from a wheelchair. She was the most ancient-looking human being I'd ever seen, but her eyes were bright and her voice surprisingly strong and youthful.

"Why, Mr. Klein! Our neighbor ran over to tell us the news. What a thing to have happen! And yet, here you are."

"Yes, ma'am," he replied in the kind of half-shout people use with the hard of hearing. "I must return to my family, but I thought you could help these gentlemen. It is important police business and might be related to the fire at my store. I hope you will assist them if you can."

"Of course. Give my love to Pearl and Esther. We will send you over some fresh bread later. Yvonne is quite the baker. But where will you be?"

"I haven't had a chance to think on it, but I expect we will move into Esther's for the time being. She and Daniel are at the hospital most of the time now anyway."

"Ah, little Alice. I heard. Such misfortunes have befallen you and yours. I shall pray for you and send Yvonne to light a candle at the cathedral if you would not be offended."

"Not at all, Mrs. Gomolka. We will accept any divine intervention we can get. I must rush. I will let these men introduce themselves, but I can vouch for them." Klein waved at us all and left with a heavy sigh to return to the scene of the disaster.

"Please sit down. You are both rather tall and it hurts my neck to look up at you."

Flanagan and I eased down on a delicate sofa across from her, crowding ourselves into the small space. We pulled our hats off and balanced them on our knees as she peered at us with curiosity.

"I'm Detective Flanagan with the City Police. This is Jim Malhaven. He's a reporter with the Crier who is, uh, assisting me in my investigation."

"Oh, yes, Mr. Malhaven. I enjoy your stories in the newspaper. You've had some strange adventures, haven't you? Must be exciting."

"Sometimes more terrifying than exciting if I'm honest, but I always appreciate a loyal reader."

"What could I possibly do for the two of you? I don't know if Mr.

Klein mentioned it, but I never leave my home, so I'm not sure what I could tell you."

Joey pulled the creased letter out of his pocket again. "Nothing too difficult. If you can read Polish, that is. We have this letter that might provide us clues to a case we're working on. May be tied into the fire at Mr. Klein's. He recognized the language and thought you would be able to translate it for us."

"How interesting. Yvonne, dear, fetch my—"

"Glasses?" the girl finished for her elderly relative, flourishing a pair of steel-rimmed lenses.

"Such a dear. You always anticipate. Now let's see what we have here." She unfolded the paper carefully. It was covered on one side only in what looked like neat handwriting from what I could tell.

"I think a woman wrote this," she said. "Men's writing is always so much messier. Hmmm…"

She perused the paper, the frown line between her eyebrows growing deeper the longer she read. When she got to the end, she crossed herself and closed her eyes.

"Are you alright, Busia?" Yvonne asked with concern.

I couldn't help jumping in too. "Is there something wrong, ma'am?"

She opened her eyes and looked hard at us. "There is a word here. I never thought to see this word again since we left the old country when I was a girl. It is a terrible story written on this paper. A story of crime and vengeance. God have mercy on the soul of the one this names, for he is likely to end up in the other place."

"Can you read it for us?"

I pulled out my notebook and took dictation as she cleared her throat and spoke haltingly as she converted the words to English in her head: "*It was Stefan. He claims it was an accident, but he has been a—* I'm not sure how you say in English. One who enjoys to set fires and watch them burn."

"An arsonist? Firebug?" I suggested.

"What a funny word—*he has been a firebug all his life. He told me he was only sixteen when he burned himself setting a barn ablaze, but the injury did not cure him of this disease, I think. And now, he has almost killed me, which would have been no great loss, but he has killed Celestyna, our precious baby, and that I cannot forgive. He told me she burnt up in the fire, but I know better. No bones were found. He has buried her, without baptism, in unconsecrated ground. She will become poroniec and walk the earth. I will save her from this fate if it is the last thing I do, but first he will pay. I write this testament as proof of my vow.* It is signed, but it is hard to make out. The ink got wet and smeared a little."

"I noticed that. What would be your best guess?" Joey asked.

"I think… yes… the Americanized version would be Nadia. Nadia Jankowski."

CHAPTER EIGHTEEN

*J*ankowski! That was another blow to the gut that nearly took my breath away. I didn't know how common a name it was among the Polish crowd, but it was yet another link to Victoria's past. I could feel Joey glance over at me, but I didn't want to meet his eye just then. Figured we could hash it out later.

He got my drift and instead asked the question that was in my mind too. "What was the word you used? Poro-something?"

She shuddered and crossed herself again. "*Poroniec.* I do not know how to translate exactly, but it is said that a baby who dies in the womb or before baptism, must be named and given burial in consecrated ground. If not, it will become a… a… bad spirit, how would you say?"

"A demon?" I suggested.

"Yes, a demon like those that live down there with the Devil," she said, pointing to the floor beneath her feet. I got the idea she wasn't talking about the residents of the first-floor apartment. "They will roam the earth, preying on women who are with child, until their remains are named and given proper burial."

"But you don't believe in that, do you, Busia?" Yvonne asked. "Sounds like the worst kind of old superstition."

"I might say so, except I saw one once when I was but a child. Before we came to America. A black-eyed, shriveled thing with wings."

Joey and I exchanged a look.

"I see you are skeptical," the old woman said, with a small smile, "but when you have lived as long as I have, nothing would surprise you anymore. *There are more things in heaven and earth…*"

"*Than are dreamt of in your philosophy*," Yvonne finished for her. "I've been studying *Hamlet*."

"Yvonne dreams of going on the stage one day. She will leave her old babcia behind and become a famous star. But she and all the young ones are quick to dismiss the traditional ways and tales. Those stories do not spring out of the ground from nothing. There is always a truth behind them."

"Well, whether this demon baby thing is real or not is beside the point, ain't it?" asked Joey. "If this woman—Nadia—believed in it, it gives her a powerful motive for tracking down our missing prisoner. He must be this Stefan she's talking about, unless we got two guys with burnt faces wandering around. And it doesn't sound like she was gonna give him a prize when she found him. She wanted vengeance for her baby."

"If she narrowly escaped being offed by him once before, maybe he decided to finish the job when she found him," I added.

"Do you think he burned down poor Mr. Klein's store? This *firebug*?" Mrs. Gomolka asked.

"Seems likely," said Flanagan. "I've arrested a few of these guys in my time. They got a fascination with fire and ain't above turning to it just for fun, not to mention settling grudges."

"But what kind of grudge did he have against Klein? We still don't know why he went to the store," I pointed out.

"Yeah, we got more questions than answers, but this was a big help, ma'am." Flanagan rose to his feet.

The old lady handed him back the letter. "I wish you good fortune. There is true evil in the world. Do not underestimate it."

With that parting shot, we took our leave and headed back toward the store.

"Jankowski," Flanagan said to me.

"I guess that's the connection, ain't it? If Nadia is his wife, maybe this Stefan is a Jankowski and a relative of Lukasz."

"Who what? Waits six or seven years after his death to come visit Lukasz's widow, who he so far hasn't made any attempt to contact that we know of. In fact, he turned tail and ran when he saw her."

"Victoria became heir to a fortune all of a sudden last fall. It was a huge story what with the murders and the drug operation. Made all the nationals, maybe the international papers for all we know. Suppose he sees the story, makes the connection and wants to hit her up for some of the windfall. Play on her sympathy as a long-lost relative of her husband, but his wife follows him to town threatening vengeance. She's bound to spill her story to Victoria if she finds out hubby's scheme, just to put a spoke in his wheel. Stefan loses the sympathy vote and his chance of a handout, so Nadia has to go. He drugs himself to work up to the deed and then… well, does whatever he did to Nadia before he's knocked out by his own poison and gets caught."

"And the photos?"

"He meets up with Lukasz over in Europe during the war. Lukasz hands him the photos, says look at the beautiful wife I got waiting for me back home. Forgets to get them back before he ships out."

"People weren't exactly knocking all around Europe back then, you know. There was a war going on."

"Well, maybe Stefan's in England for some reason. Lukasz worked the North Atlantic route on a ship ferrying soldiers over from New York. Easy enough for them to meet up there."

"Maybe, but the Krauts and Commies had shut down Poland before that. Unless he and his wife got out, he wouldn't have been allowed to travel, would he?"

"I don't know. Would he? You gotta remember, I was in the South Pacific the whole time. I'm no expert on what was going on all the way around the other side of the world, but I bet that's the kind of thing Q could research for us."

"You'll have to be the one to ask him—he don't like me none. It's not a bad theory. Stefan going after a piece of the Wynter pie. Money's at the bottom of most crime. But it don't explain the delay in hooking up with Mrs. J after he got to town. Why waste money on a fleabag motel room when he could've marched right up to the Wynter mansion and asked for a bed? Victoria would've thrown the door wide for any long lost relative of her hubby, wouldn't she?"

"Sure, but he wasn't to know that. Maybe he chickened out or was working up his nerve and then things went south before he got a chance. Now he's a man on the run. Not the best time to announce to someone 'I'm the long-lost cousin-in-law you never heard of.'"

"I guess there's something in it, but it's got some holes."

"Most stories don't make sense until you got all the facts. We just gotta fill in the background."

We'd made it back to Klein's store by this time. The crowd had dwindled some so we had no trouble spotting Victoria and the Kleins sitting on a stoop across from the burnt-out remains.

"Did you have any luck, gentlemen?" Klein asked.

"Yeah," I said. "Mrs. Gomolka was a pip. Translated the letter for us in no time flat. Gave us a whole new lead."

"I am glad Dame Fortune has smiled on your efforts. I'm afraid she has turned her back on me and mine."

"Don't say that, Papa," Esther said. She was a pretty, dark-haired woman, but the strain she'd been under showed on her face. "We need all the good thoughts we can get with Alice in the hospital. You'll rebuild the store. In the meantime, you and Mama will come and stay with us. The rest of the kids'll love it. They don't see enough of you, you're always so busy working on your hats."

"It will be a long time before I am so busy again. Perhaps never. Maybe this is a sign to give up the business and retire."

"Don't, Papa. I know it seems like we are under a bad sign with Alice and the store and Daniel—"

"What about Daniel?" asked Victoria. "You didn't mention he had trouble."

"Oh, so much going on, I'd almost forgotten myself, but he was crossing the road the day Alice got sick and was struck by a taxicab. He might have died! And the worst thing was, all the witnesses said the taxi aimed right at him. Almost as if someone wanted him dead! Can you imagine?"

CHAPTER NINETEEN

"I remember the case," said Flanagan. "Hit and run."

Esther agreed. "Yes. One of the witnesses got the cab number, but it turned out it had been stolen from the driver only a few minutes earlier."

"That's right. They found it abandoned later. Was your husband hurt bad?"

"Terribly bruised and sore, but they checked him out at the hospital after we brought Alice in and thank goodness it was nothing worse. I don't know what I would have done if I had lost him, and then Alice getting so sick. We do seem to be under a dark cloud, but things could always be worse."

"I suppose that's true," I said, "but it does seem a weird coincidence someone tried to run down your husband and burned your father's store to the ground all within the space of a week."

Figuring it was time to let them in on what we'd found out, I glanced over at Joey. He gave me the nod to go ahead and spill the beans.

"I don't know how much Victoria told you, but there was a woman found dead at the movie palace yesterday. A guy with a burned face was found passed out there too. The letter the detective showed you,

Mr. Klein, was found in the dead woman's suitcase. Let me read you the translation the way Mrs. Gomolka told it to us."

I took out my notebook and read my shorthand to the crowd.

"Poor woman," said Victoria. "It sounds as if she had been through an ordeal and then to die so young. Do you think this Stefan is responsible for her death?"

"We gotta consider it," said Joey. "We don't have a definite cause of death yet, but this guy obviously ain't acting on the up and up, what with all this running around and making himself scarce. She says in the letter he's a firebug, and now we got an unexplained fire. Seems an obvious explanation to me."

"But why target Mr. Klein? And what about the photograph of Lukasz and me? What possible connection could there be?"

"Jimmy didn't read you the signature on the letter. That's the connection. It's signed Nadia Jankowski."

"Jankowski! Do you think she was a relative of Lukasz? Is that how she got the photograph?"

"She coulda been, or more likely her husband was, assuming she took his name when they married. She was wearing a wedding band."

"But that doesn't answer why this man would target us," Esther said. "We were friends with Lukasz, of course, but he passed so long ago. None of this makes sense."

"We're thinking maybe he found out about Victoria coming into money," I said. "He might've thought she'd take pity on a relative of Lukasz's. Cut him in for a share. But if that's his motive, what he's been doing since he got here is a mystery. He's been acting like a desperate man, and a guilty one, with all these shenanigans, but we're missing the thread that ties it all together."

Victoria looked more than troubled at these revelations. "It's hard not to feel as though this is all my fault. That woman's death, Daniel, and now Mr. Klein's store. How much more trouble will this man cause, and for what? To somehow profit from my inheritance? I've always felt the Wynter fortune is cursed. It was ill-gotten gains to begin with and seems to ruin everything it touches. If Aunt Livinia didn't have control over it, I would give it all away. It isn't worth this heartache."

I wrapped her up in my arms. "Don't, honey. Even if this is connected to Lukasz, it's nobody's fault what's happened but this nut Stefan. Sounds like he's been a rotten egg his whole life."

"But he wouldn't even be here if it weren't for my connection to Lukasz. What do you think he'll do next?"

"If he's smart—which we got no evidence to suggest he is at this point—he would beat it back to whatever rock he crawled out from under. No matter what his plan was, I don't think it's panned out the way he expected. Seems as though he's in way over his head. I don't see what he could hope to gain by sticking around except a shiny pair of steel bracelets when Joey and I catch up with him. But it might be smart to keep an eye on all of you in case he ain't that bright."

"Just what I was thinking, Jimmy," Flanagan said. "I'll assign a couple of experienced beat cops to the Kleins. Why don't you stick close to Mrs. Jankowski? Don't expect you'll find that assignment a hardship."

"Not a bit, Joey, not a bit. If we stop by the paper, I got time to get a description of the guy in the afternoon edition. That way the whole town'll be looking out for him. With a kisser like his, he's got no more chance of escaping notice than I do. Assuming that meets with your approval, Detective?"

"Sure. At this point, we gotta pull out all the stops to find this guy. He's a one-man crime wave. Can't have him setting fires and running down upstanding citizens all over town. But like you said, if he's smart, he's long gone. At the very least, he's probably laying low until darkness falls again. I'd love to get my mitts on him before that happens."

Victoria parted ways with the Kleins amid tears, hugs, and promises to do what she could to help them out. They were a proud family, so I couldn't see them accepting money from her, but there's plenty of other ways to assist friends in need. Like finding the villain that put them in such a tough spot and bringing him to heel.

We stopped by the Crier. This time it was Victoria's turn to visit with Q and fill him in on the latest developments, while I typed up a column for the next edition that made Morty plenty happy. He wasn't a ghoul, but what editor wouldn't salivate over such a juicy story as arson and attempted murder? That's the kind of headlines sells papers like half-price hotcakes.

I made my way down to the morgue and rehashed the facts with Q and Victoria.

"Mrs. Jankowski's husband does seem to be the connection between all these events," Q observed. "If this man is a relative, it might explain why he and the woman we're presuming was his wife had the photographs."

"Joey and I were discussing that," I said. "Lukasz's family came from Poland, and the letter on the woman was in Polish, but that doesn't mean they were living in Poland during the war, does it? They might have made their way to England with other refugees or even been living there before the war started. Whatever country he was in, this Stefan was probably excused from serving in the army because of his injuries."

"We might be able to track down a record if he and his wife were living in England at the outbreak of war. Every household member was required to register in 1939. They were issued identification cards to help track casualties from the bombings and attempt to keep out foreign infiltrators."

"Is that right? How do you happen to know that?"

"I've studied a lot about the war. I turned 18 as the fighting was ending. Too late to do my part unfortunately."

"Well, you may still get a chance to serve. Things are popping over on the Korean peninsula. I heard they ain't gonna force vets from the last war to fight if hostilities break out. I'm no coward, but I've had enough of that to last a lifetime."

"I'm registered for the draft, of course. My mother and sister have been worried about me being called up. The situation there is very confusing, isn't it?"

"Don't seem as straightforward as the last one, that's for sure. That was a case of kill or be killed. I don't pretend to understand all this geopolitical whatsit people talk about nowadays. Seems like a chess game being played by world leaders that's gonna get a lot of good people on the ground killed, but I guess like most things, it's out of the hands of us regular joes."

"Yes," Q agreed. "I'll go if I'm called, but I don't think I'll volunteer unless it continues to escalate. I've heard stories that black soldiers aren't being treated much better these days even though they are supposed to be desegregating the troops."

"Ha, I'll believe that when I see it. There's no place sticks to tradition like the military in my experience. But we've gotten off subject. You think you can check on that census in England? Would be interesting to know if this Stefan and Nadia Jankowski were listed."

"I've got some contacts I can telegraph or even telephone, but I don't know if the paper would appreciate the cost of overseas calls."

"You can send the bill to me," Victoria spoke up. "It feels like there's no time to lose. I'll be holding my breath until we discover what this man wants and put a stop to his crimes."

I couldn't help but grin. "That don't sound like the best idea, sweetheart. You might pass out. It could very well be days before we find this goon, much less find out what he's up to."

As was not an unusual occurrence, I would turn out to be wrong on both counts. When will I ever learn?

CHAPTER TWENTY

*L*eaving Q to start placing calls with the international operator, we headed back home. I was used to being clean-shaven. All that itchy stubble against my scar was getting on my nerves. I insisted on Victoria hanging out at the cottage while I got cleaned up. Wasn't going to make the mistake of letting her out of shouting distance with that crook on the loose.

We strolled up to the big house together and indulged in a combo breakfast and lunch with scrambled eggs, bacon, and a spiced tomato soup that was one of Mr. Cressley's specialties. He sat down to join us at the big kitchen table.

Even Liv deigned to join the crew, her curiosity about the morning's events beating out her sense of proper decorum for the lady of the house. "Shocking! Absolutely shocking that a merchant of Mr Klein's long standing in the community should be targeted in this way. And there's a possibility this man might be a relative of Victoria's husband? I don't enjoy suggesting it, but this may be what comes of marrying beneath oneself," Liv added, with a rather pointed look at yours truly.

"Says the woman who married her butler," I blurted out before Victoria even had a chance to defend herself.

I felt bad the minute I said it. Cressley was a good guy. Better than his wife in most ways. He was the one who'd stooped to conquer in that relationship. Cressley looked like he was trying not to smirk, but Liv turned the same color of puce as her blouse.

Victoria surprised me by laying a hand on her aunt's. "Lukasz was the kindest and sweetest man I ever knew, and I was a penniless orphan at the time, Aunt Livinia. We were lucky to have each other. I never thought I'd meet a man with as big a heart until Jim happened into my life. There aren't many women so lucky as to find a second chance. I think you know better than anyone that it's what's inside a person that matters more than their perceived importance in the world."

"Humph," was Liv's only reply, but she didn't try and challenge it.

I marveled again at Victoria's patience with her aunt, who had to be one of the most maddening dames I'd ever run across. I guess knowing what Livinia had been through with her father and sisters gave Victoria sympathy and a desire to extend grace to the woman that I couldn't always muster myself.

"The important thing is we find this man," Victoria continued. "If he is related to Lukasz, I want to talk to him regardless of what he's done. He may know of other relatives I could get in touch with. Even though Lukasz is gone, he was an important part of my life. It would be fascinating to find out more about his Polish origins. I know his parents came over when they married, hoping to find a better life here, but they both died relatively young, before I met him. You don't realize how important family is until you have none."

I had to agree. Except for Joey, I was pretty much a loner in the world before I met Victoria. Since the events that had first brought us together, my circle of friends and acquaintances had expanded by quite a bit one way and another. Gotta admit it felt good to think there were a few more folks around who might care if I lived or died.

Flanagan called as we were clearing up the kitchen to report there was nothing much to report. No sightings of the mystery man, but the afternoon edition of the Crier was just hitting the streets. We were hopeful enlisting the eyes of the good citizens of Carsworth City would help us flush out our quarry.

I debated running back into town to help with the search but wanted to stick close to Victoria in case. I decided to get a little work done around the cemetery instead. There were enough people keeping an eye out in town, and there was always plenty of cleaning up to do around the boneyard.

Victoria had hired a couple of kids, Mabel and Mikey Cummings, to help on the weekends. Their parents had decided to produce the biggest brood of children the city had ever known, so they could use the extra cash. Not to mention getting two of their kiddies out from under foot once in a while was a bonus. Mabel was a whiz kid in anything she did. Even though she'd been born and raised in the city, she'd learned the difference between weeds and flowers in no time at all. She was also a mechanical genius who'd fixed the old lawnmower Liv was too stingy to replace twice already just since they started.

Mikey was a different story, however. It's not often Victoria and I had a serious disagreement, but when I heard she'd invited that hooligan to join our crew, we came as close as we ever had to a knock-down, drag-out fight. She felt sorry for the kid as he can't seem to avoid trouble, but she hadn't had the hair-raising experiences I'd suffered whenever that motormouth was around. As expected, he talked more than he worked, but Mabel mostly took him in charge and kept him away from me and out of danger. Although, there was an incident with the rose pruners that we won't dwell on.

I started collecting branches that had fallen in one of those summer squalls that blows through from time to time and was making a pile to burn later when I caught sight of Archie acting funny. He was doing that weird sideways walk cats do when they're riled up, with his tail puffed up to at least twice its normal size.

Sure, a lot of places have watchdogs, but Archie was a pretty fair watchcat. He kept an eye out on the cemetery and patrolled the grounds regular, so I always paid attention when he was upset. Usually, it was a rival cat who'd wandered onto the grounds or one of the squirrels who liked to tease him, but once, it'd been the biggest copperhead I ever seen, so I wandered over to investigate and make sure Archie didn't get too close to whatever it was.

The cat was hissing at one of the angel statues on the grounds.

Angels being a popular theme for monuments, we had our fair share, but this one was my favorite. It stood back from the headstone with wings drawn around in a circle and its body half bent over as though it was protecting the grave from harm. Too late for the young girl buried there, but it happened to form a convenient hiding place for wildlife. I'd more than once flushed out a sleepy possum or grumbling raccoon.

This time, there was slightly bigger game. I spied one bare foot before I saw the rest of him. Guess he hadn't had any luck in picking up a new pair of shoes since we last seen him riding away on that bus in town. I nudged the foot with my big hoof. The guy reared up like a jack-in-the-box, banging his head hard on the underside of the angel as he stepped out.

"Careful, there," I advised. "That's a valuable statue."

I was ready to leap, figuring he'd run off like a startled hare, but he surprised me by standing his ground. We held a staring contest for a minute, but I'm easily bored so I broke the silence.

"Lot of people looking for you in town. Whatchu doing out here?"

He cleared his throat. When he spoke, there was a hoarse rasp to his voice that sounded permanent. I figured it was damage from the same fire that wrecked his face. "I need to see Victoria Jankowski. I can explain everything."

"Everything as in killing your wife and baby, evading the police, running down innocent citizens, and burning up a fine haberdashery establishment?"

"You've got it all wrong. I have been running from the police, but only because they seemed to think I killed Nadia. I swear I didn't, but I know they won't believe me. I need a good lawyer and don't have the money to pay for one. If I can speak to Victoria, I'm sure she'll want to help me."

"Here's your chance," I said, keeping a wary eye on the guy in case he tried anything. "She's walking down here right this minute."

He turned to see what I could see, Victoria threading her way through the gravestones to find out who I was talking to. I could tell the minute she got close enough to recognize that it was the guy from Klein's shop. There was a slight change in her expression that wouldn't have been noticeable to anyone who hadn't memorized her every feature the way I had. She knew how to keep her cool.

He didn't have any weapon that I could see, and I was bigger than him, but I kept a watchful eye anyway in case he had any bright ideas about hurting Victoria once she got close. She joined me, hooking one hand inside my arm so that we presented a united front.

"I saw we had a visitor, but I must say, a most unexpected one. Stefan Jankowski, I presume?"

"Yes, that is, no, that is—it's complicated. God, it's good to see you. I've missed you so much, you wouldn't believe."

"Missed me? Have we met before?"

"Of course we have. I know I've changed—my voice and my face, but don't you know me? Daisy, it's me. It's Lukasz."

CHAPTER TWENTY-ONE

ictoria's hand tightened on my bicep at the words. I wasn't sure if she was more shocked at his claim to be Lukasz, or at his use of the old nickname only her husband had ever called her, but she didn't miss a beat.

"Lukasz is dead."

"No, no, I'm not. It's a long story, but you have to believe me. I'm Lukasz Jankowski."

Gotta admit, my stomach dropped down to the vicinity of my feet at the idea Lukasz was alive and well, but I had questions. "Where you been all this time then? And how'd you end up with another wife?"

"Nadia wasn't my wife. That is, she thought she was, but it's a long story, and I'm afraid the police are gonna track me down any minute. I need a guarantee from you I'll get a good lawyer. I can explain everything, but not if they lock me away."

"That's the best time and place to explain things," I said. "Nothing cops enjoy more than a good confession."

"But it'll sound crazy to them. You know me, Daisy. You'll understand."

"Don't call me that," Victoria said, her voice harsh and flat. "That was something special between me and Lukasz. From what we can gather, you're a murderer and an arsonist. Don't sully his memory by trying to convince anybody that you're someone you can't even hold a candle to."

"I swear. I swear. And I can prove it too."

He wrestled the wedding ring from his finger and offered it to us. I grabbed it and handed it to Victoria. She held it up to her eye so she could see the engraving on the inside.

"Where did you get this and the photographs? Did you steal them?"

"What is it, honey?" I asked. "Are you saying it belonged to Lukasz?"

"It looks like his ring. We couldn't afford a long inscription, but we had our initials added." She handed me the ring.

I could just make out the "VJ" and "LJ" engraved on the thin band. "Don't look so distinctive. Anybody could get that put on a ring," I said, handing it back to him.

"But it's ours," he insisted, slipping it back on. "You put it on my finger the day we were married. You wore the dress with the cherries. The same as the photos we took. Esther lent you a bracelet with blue enamel for luck, and I bought you a big bunch of white daisies. They cost a fortune because it was out of season, but I wanted you to have something special."

Victoria wasn't buying it. "Those are all details Lukasz could have told you. Who are you? A cousin? Did you meet up with Lukasz when he was on shore leave in England and pump him for information about me? No, knowing Lukasz, you probably didn't have to. He always talked far too much about me to anyone he met but then, we were in love, so I did as well. That's what young lovers do, don't they? Bore the world with their romance. I bet Nadia used to brag about you, unless she'd already found out what you really were."

"I'm telling you I can prove all this. I got all the letters you sent me and my ID papers."

"How'd you hang on to all that stuff?" I objected. "It would've all gone down with the ship."

"I'd left it on shore accidentally the last time we sailed. Left it at a friend's house. They hung on to it for me until I could collect it."

"None of this explains where you been all these years if you really were Lukasz. His ship went down almost seven years ago now. The Navy thinks you're at the bottom of the ocean. Or are you gonna tell us you, or Lukasz I should say, wasn't on the boat when it got sunk."

"Of course I was on board. After the torpedo struck, half of the ship was on fire. I was trying to help some of the men get up on deck when I got burned myself. I think something must have hit me because next thing I knew, I was on a medical ship. I'd lost my tags somehow and I was confused. I couldn't rememb—"

"Don't say it. Don't bring up that old amnesia gag," I scoffed, growing more and more convinced this was all a scam.

"I know it sounds unlikely, but I was a medic. I'd seen it happen to other sailors with head injuries. The Navy transferred me to a hospital in London for specialty treatment for my burns. I was in so much pain at first. You can't imagine what it's like, these kind of burns. Every nerve in your body screams."

"You ain't faking the burns. Anyone can see that. Don't prove you got 'em the way you say you got 'em. Nadia left a letter. Said you'd done it to yourself trying to burn a barn down when you was a kid."

"That's what I told her when I met her. My burns were healed as well as they were going to by then. I didn't want to tell her the real story."

"Why not? A war hero—what girl don't love that?"

"I didn't want to have to explain who I really was to her, so I panicked and made up a story when she asked me."

"So, you had remembered who you were," Victoria said. "That's the biggest proof of all you're lying. If you were Lukasz and had lost your memory, when you realized who you were, the first thing you'd have done would be to let me know and come back to me."

"I wanted to, believe me I did. But look at my face. I see the winces I get from other people when I walk past them on the street. I'm not the man you married. I thought you deserved better."

"I don't believe one word of this. Lukasz and I had a relationship that went much deeper than mere physical appearance. He would have come back to me, and he would have known he'd be welcome no matter what injuries or scars he'd collected."

"Yeah, I'm proof of that," I couldn't help saying. "Any woman who could see past my ugly kisser to want to marry me wouldn't be put off by much."

"But you can't get married," the guy objected. "She already has a husband."

"That didn't seem to stop you from picking up an extra wife."

"Like I said, Nadia wasn't my wife. I'll admit I had relations with her that I shouldn't, but I was lonely and flattered. I didn't think any woman would ever look at me again the way she did. But then she found out she was going to have a baby, and her father pressured me to marry her. I couldn't explain I was already married. Her father would've killed me. So I hired a guy to pretend he was a priest and marry us, but it wasn't real. It was just to make her happy."

"And the baby?" Victoria asked softly.

"There was an accident. A fire. Nadia was able to get out, but she left the baby behind. It seemed to break something in her mind. She accused me of setting the fire. Used that story I told her about burning down a barn as proof. Her family was important in the town where we were living. I was afraid for my life, so I ran. I didn't know what to do, so I decided it was time to come home."

"That's convenient," I said. "Was this about the time Victoria came into a bunch of money?"

"I did see a story in the paper about what happened with her mother, but I didn't think about the money. I thought she might need some support after going through such a terrible thing. And I'll admit, I wanted to get as far away as possible from Nadia and her family."

"But she followed you here, didn't she? That was kinda awkward to say the least. Lucky for you she didn't survive too long after she got here. Very lucky."

"I know it looks bad, but I swear I don't know what happened. She contacted me and we arranged to meet at the theater. When I got there, I found her dead already in her seat."

"And we found you passed out."

"I miscalculated my pain dosage. Probably because I was so nervous about meeting her. I started feeling it when I found her. All I could think was to get out of there, but I didn't make it. I woke up in the hospital with cops telling me I killed Nadia and I—"

"Panicked?" I suggested. "You seem to do a lot of that."

He ignored my witticism. "Victoria, I need your help. I'm gonna need a good lawyer to get out of this."

"Why on earth would I help you?"

"I know I've changed. My face, my voice…"

"The thing that doesn't change is who a person is. None of what you've described is the way Lukasz would ever have behaved in a thousand years. He certainly wouldn't have burned down Mr. Klein's store."

"That was nothing to do with me. I wanted to talk to him. I didn't want to spring myself on you. I thought maybe Mr. Klein could contact you, let you know I was here. Why would I want to burn down a hat store?"

A lightbulb went off over my head. I could only think of one reason.

"I thought of a quick way to test out whether you're Lukasz or not," I said, pulling my fedora down from my head and popping it on to his melon before he knew what was what. It promptly swallowed the top half of his head, coming to rest on what was left of the bridge of his nose.

"That hat don't fit you near as well as it used to, does it?"

CHAPTER TWENTY-TWO

"I don't know what you're talking about," he protested. "Why should your hat fit me?"

"Because that self-same hat was custom made for Lukasz Jankowski on the happy occasion of his marriage. Later gifted to me by his widow and happened to fit me like a glove, which was quite a thing as there are all different head sizes and shapes, ain't they? I wouldn't be at all surprised if a superior artist such as Mr. Klein didn't keep detailed records on every hat he'd ever made, including head measurements. There's a lot changes about a man over the years, but I never heard of anyone's skull shrinking that much before, burns or no burns."

Victoria laughed. "Oh, Jim, you can be brilliant sometimes, can't you?"

I preened a bit, thinking I'd stumbled upon a fact that would shut the guy up, but I guess he was desperate because he just blurted out, "Tell the cops to check under the floor in my hotel room. There's proof there." Then he took off running, hat and all.

That made me plenty mad seeing as how I was fond of my hat, so I took off after him with Victoria not far behind. We must have looked crazy to anyone watching from the house as the three of us zigzagged around the monuments. I always try to be respectful about walking over the graves, but in the heat of the moment, all bets were off.

He made it as far as the big stone wall that runs along the front of the cemetery grounds before we caught up to him. I thought for sure we had him, but then a bunch of things happened at once. He hoisted himself up onto a headstone and got one leg over the top of the wall. The hat fell off, which I must admit both relieved and distracted me as I automatically bent down to reclaim it. And a huge black bat—yes, I said a bat—appeared out of nowhere making a weird scritching noise and dove at Victoria's face.

She sprang back more in surprise than fear and stumbled over a marker, landing with a sickening-sounding thud on the ground. All thought of catching the guy flew out of my mind. He could run to Timbuktu as far as I was concerned. My only thought was for Victoria.

"Honey! Are you okay?"

"Oof, I don't know," she said in a low whisper. "Knocked the breath out of me."

"Take it easy. Does it hurt anywhere?"

She closed her eyes. "I don't think anything's broken, but give me a minute. You should run after him. Don't let him get away."

"Forget it. He won't go far. He really seems to think you're gonna gift him with a lawyer to get out of this mess."

"He can think again on that. It made me so angry to hear him pretending to be Lukasz. I could have scratched his eyes out."

"Kind of like that thing just tried to do to you."

"What was it?" Victoria asked.

"I don't know. It happened so fast, it was kind of blurry. It looked to me like some kind of bat."

"I've never seen a bat around here that big and never during the day before. Are you sure it wasn't some kind of bird? A raven or crow?"

"Looked bigger than that. And leathery wings, not feathers. Creepy-looking."

"Reminds me of what Mrs. Gomolka said to you. About that demon baby."

"Now don't start. I'm all washed up with the supernatural hocus-pocus. What we got here is a regular, garden-variety flimflam artist trying to take advantage of the woman I love, and I won't stand for it."

"You don't have to worry about me. Lukasz and I knew each other through and through. That man is nothing like him in any way. I can't believe he thinks I'd fall for such a ruse. If he had only come here as a relative of Lukasz's, I would have been happy to help him."

"His kind don't think that way. Probably thought it was a surefire plan what with his burns and all. Hard to prove it isn't Lukasz if he's got papers. Maybe he thought you'd be so lonely, you'd be willing to accept any story."

"I hate this, Jim. I feel as though he's sullying my happy memories of Lukasz and bringing up all the bad ones again."

I helped her sit up, sitting down beside her on the ground and supporting her against my chest. "Don't let a cheat like that get to you. We'll let Flanagan know he's still around. They'll catch him soon and put him away for this crime spree he's been on."

"Do you really think he burned down Mr. Klein's store simply to hide any records?"

"Seems farfetched, I guess, but don't forget about Esther's husband almost getting run down. Maybe that's what he's been doing since he got to town. Figuring out who might have known Lukasz well enough to have an opinion on whether he was back from the dead. You said Daniel and Lukasz were pretty close."

"His family took Lukasz in after his parents died. They were as close as brothers. He'll see right through this fraud as quickly as I did."

"See, that's a pretty good motive for getting rid of Daniel then. Like I said, if he's got papers and other supposed proof, it's not out of the question Stefan could convince a judge to rule that he is Lukasz. The less evidence there is pointing in another direction, the better chance he has."

"The hat didn't fit. That's evidence."

"Yeah, bet he didn't know you'd hung on to Lukasz's hat, much less donated it to yours truly. But I'm not sure it's the kind of thing that'd hold up in a court of law if it came to that."

"It does seem as though he must have met Lukasz. He could forge identification papers, but letters in my handwriting, if he really has them, and those photographs he could only have gotten from Lukasz."

"Yeah, and what about the ring? I'm a mug. I should've hung on to it. We might have been able to get a jeweler to compare the engraving with yours."

"That's a good idea," she said, jumping to her feet. "When they catch him, we can still do it. For the moment, we need to let Detective Flanagan know what's happened."

I groaned, regretting my impulsive decision to sit down on the ground. I wasn't an old man yet, but sometimes I felt like one. Victoria held out her hands and helped me hoist myself up.

She wrapped her arms around me in a fierce hug once I was vertical again.

"What's this?" I asked, returning the favor.

"I'm thinking about our wedding. This is casting a pall over what should be a joyous time for us. Maybe we should think about postponing getting married. Who knows how long it will take to catch Stefan and prove he's lying? I know he's not Lukasz, but if the story gets out, what will the rest of the world think of me rushing into marriage with another man? I'm assuming you'll eventually have to write about the connection to me for the paper. You won't be able to sit on that part of the story much longer."

I reared back so I could look her in the eye. "You know I'd quit my job in a minute rather than do anything to harm you."

"But that wouldn't be fair to you. I know you love writing for the paper. And if you don't write the story, one of the other reporters will. I just don't want Lukasz's good name dragged through the mud. If people believe Stefan is him, they might believe he's done all these terrible things too, unless Stefan was telling the truth about not being involved in them."

"That would be a lot for me to swallow. A coincidence is just a coincidence but when you start getting two, three, four stacked up, that's a pattern. If we don't find this guy is responsible for the mayhem that's been going on since he got to town, I will eat this self-same hat with steak sauce and horseradish," I added, flourishing my chapeau.

"Oh, dear, we'll hope it doesn't come to that. Sounds like a recipe for indigestion," she said with a smile.

"That's more like it. You know I love to see you smile. Try not to worry. We've got over a week to go before we're scheduled to stand before the judge. This will all be settled way before then, you wait and see."

"I hope you're right."

"Ain't I always?"

"No."

She had a point.

CHAPTER TWENTY-THREE

In news that will come as no surprise to you, it turned out Victoria had a better grasp on the likelihood of everything settling down quick than I did. I thought we'd catch the guy and get a confession out of him in just a day or two. Starry-eyed optimist, that's me. Instead, it turned into a waiting game as all signs of Stefan Jankowski dried up. Either he'd left town or had found an ace hideout.

Flanagan recovered the letters and ID papers from the hotel room. Found them under a loose floorboard beneath the bed and brought them out to the cemetery to show Victoria. It was tough watching her sort through the letters, stopping to read one now and again, tears in her eyes. It was harder for her, seeing all those hopes and dreams and fears she and Lukasz had shared all those years ago brought to life again.

"These are mine," she had to admit. "I remember many of them so well. I used to labor over what to say for hours, not wanting to give him any cause for worry. Trying to think of cheerful details about my life here to tell him."

"I figured," Flanagan said. "Don't seem likely anyone would go to the trouble or have the skill to forge this many letters. The ID papers are another story. Pretty standard issue. Wouldn't be hard to find someone willing to work up a false set, particularly in the hubbub after the war. There were a lot of undocumented people who'd lost their papers. Perfect time to take on a new identity without anyone asking too many questions."

"So, if the letters are real," I said, "Stefan must have gotten them from Lukasz somehow along with the photos. Either given them for safekeeping or stole them. Which likely means he did meet up with Lukasz. If Jankowski is Stefan's real name, not too hard to convince Lukasz he was a long-lost cousin, whether it's true or not. They meet up while he's on shore leave, and Lukasz can't help talking all about the most important thing in his life, his lovely wife waiting back home for him. Let's loose with details like his nickname for her and all about their wedding day."

Victoria had an objection to that line of thought. "But I was a nobody then. A poor orphan working as a cemetery caretaker. Why would he even bother to remember the things Lukasz said about me? There would have been no advantage to trying to convince me he was my husband then. And he had no way of knowing Lukasz would be killed, opening the way for him to try to take over his identity."

"True, unless he had an idea of taking care of Lukasz himself. Let's think this through. Did Lukasz ever mention anything about trying to contact relatives when he was overseas?"

"We had talked about it. How if he had a chance, he would love to meet some of his parents' relations, but we both thought it unlikely. If they were still in Poland, there seemed no chance of contacting them with the country being under German and Russian control."

"It might hinge on whether Stefan was living in England. Q's working on that end of things with his overseas contacts. But if he was living there, maybe it was as simple as Lukasz looking him up in a phone book. How many Jankowskis could there be? Calls a few to see, and Stefan is the one he happens to connect with."

"And leaves my letters and the photos with him after just meeting him?"

"That part is murky unless, like I said, Stefan already had an idea in mind of trading identities. Nadia claimed he was a firebug who couldn't resist doing it. Maybe he was in trouble and saw a way out by becoming someone else. Stole the stuff to bolster his case."

"Are you saying he was planning to kill Lukasz and take over his life?" Flanagan said. "What was he gonna do? Report for duty on the ship with a burnt face, assuming he'd already been injured, and think no one would notice?"

"Maybe he just wanted Lukasz's ID papers, then disappears. Plans to travel over to America at some point and start a new life, not necessarily with Victoria, but it doesn't pan out. Then, years later, he sees Victoria has come into some serious moolah. The temptation is too much. He decides to seek her out. Knows it's gonna be a tough sell, so he tries to muddy the waters by eliminating witnesses and evidence. Only he ain't very good at it. Whatever he's up to, I think we can agree this joker is no criminal mastermind. Everything he touches turns to mud. Some guys are unlucky that way."

"When does he find out Lukasz is dead, though?" Victoria asked.

"It was in all the stories about you last year how you was a widow because Lukasz died in service to his country. That's the kind of tug at your heartstrings angle reporters always play up, and I should know."

"But that would imply he didn't take over Lukasz's identity immediately but hung on to the letters and papers all these years. And Nadia knew him as Stefan not Lukasz."

Flanagan spoke up again. "Maybe just an insurance policy, hanging on to the stuff. In case he ever needed to disappear, and it looks like he did after this fire his wife talked about and the baby dying. He left her behind like he was trying to make an escape. Don't seem as if he expected her to follow him all the way over here and spoil his plans."

Victoria gave him a cynical look. "You men always underestimate the determination of a woman who feels wronged, particularly if he did something that led to the death of her child. I would hound someone to the ends of the earth."

"Yeah," Joey agreed, "and we still don't know what Nadia died of. Doc said the tests didn't detect poison, but it seems pretty fishy a young woman like that, with vengeance on her mind, just happens to kick off. Couldn't find anything in her belongings to suggest she was taking any medications or had a heart problem."

"That reminds me," I said. "Wasn't there a locker key found with the woman's stuff along with a train ticket?"

"We're working on that. Definitely looks like it's from the kind of locker found in train stations, but the train she took was no express line. She probably couldn't afford it. It stopped a million places between here and there. She could've jumped off and left something at any of the stations. It's gonna take a long time to check them all out."

"Sounds like the train I took to New York to visit with Lukasz while he was on shore leave," Victoria said. "The trip took over twenty hours and certainly made a lot of stops. It was the last time I ever saw him," she added softly.

Joey patted her shoulder awkwardly. "That's tough. It's not right this fella trying to take advantage of you. We're gonna find him, and then maybe we'll finally get to the bottom of all this. Our theories right now got more holes in them than Swiss cheese, and he's the only one with the answers we need."

Flanagan took his leave after making me promise to keep the Lukasz angle out of the papers for now. That wasn't hard as I was not eager to put Victoria back into the spotlight until we had to. Our wedding date was only a couple of days away now, and I had a sinking feeling all this was gonna somehow prevent me from marrying the love of my life.

We discussed putting it off. We were only going to the City Courthouse after all, then have people back to the house for an informal party after. It's not as though we had a church and banquet hall reserved and hundreds of guests invited or anything. If it was up to Victoria, we probably would've waited. She didn't want any dark clouds hanging over us on our wedding day, but I was more stubborn about it. I believed Victoria's instincts. She knew one hundred percent her husband was dead and buried at sea. Why delay because of some imposter running around the city claiming otherwise?

I'll admit I let off steam about the guy plenty to anyone who was in on the secret. I was more than a little irritated and embarrassed he'd slipped through my hands twice. I swore if I laid eyes on him again, he wouldn't be so lucky, and I didn't care what I had to do to persuade him to turn himself in to the cops.

Flanagan asked me to stay out of the way of the official investigation, but we met up most nights to stay in touch on the progress or lack of. I kept spinning it out in the paper as much as I could, doing follow up stories on the Kleins and speculation about the accident with Esther's husband. That story brought in a witness who hadn't come forward before to give a description of the man driving the stolen cab. Not surprisingly, it matched up with Stefan Jankowski to a T.

I also kept my ear to the ground, alert for any unusual happenings around the city. Reported on a couple of minor fires that turned out to be easily explained by food left on the stove too long or an overloaded electrical outlet. I was in the bullpen shooting the breeze with Maudie when another fire call came in. It wasn't far away so I hoofed it over. Was surprised to see Flanagan on the scene. Fires don't usually rate senior police detectives unless there's something suspicious about them.

He caught sight of me and waved me over past the barricades set up on the street to keep back the neck-craning crowd. He was standing in front of a building that looked derelict. Weren't many like it in town as times had been booming since the end of the war, but it had a for sale sign stuck in the window, so I guess it was waiting for a new owner to rehabilitate it.

"What's the story?" I asked Joey. "Corner the guy?"

"In a manner of speaking. Another fire, but this ain't your usual. Come take a look."

I followed him up a flight of wooden stairs, worn and scarred by a lotta years of foot traffic, to an open door at the top. I could smell the smoke before I got there and another stench I hadn't smelled since the war, but I knew it right off. It was the unmistakably oily stink of roasted flesh. Human flesh.

CHAPTER TWENTY-FOUR

I wasn't sure what to expect when I walked into the room. What I got looked like the inside of a trash bin, with crumpled newspapers, old food, and a stained mattress taking up floor space. There was what looked as though it used to be a worn-out armchair sitting in one corner, but there was hardly enough left to be sure. Sitting upright in it looked to be the outline of what was once a human being, but all that was left, I kid you not, was a greasy pile of ash and a pair of bare feet.

The rest of the room was relatively untouched except for some smoke damage to the ceiling above the body. There was a persistent stink that was enough to make us all pull out our handkerchiefs and cover our noses and mouths to try and tone it down enough to breathe.

A burly guy in a fireman's coat and hat walked over to us. I recognized him as Mike Reilly, a chief in the city fire department.

"Weird, ain't it?" he remarked, and we could hardly disagree with his astute assessment. "I seen a picture of this once in the fire journal we get at the station. Spontaneous human combustion, it's called."

"Is that what it sounds like?" Flanagan asked.

"Yep, body bursts into flame and burns hot and fast, feeding on its own fat like a candle does on wax. You end up with a dead person but not much damage to the rest of the joint just as we see here."

"Must be something to spark it though," I said. "Cigarette or match."

"Could've been, but if so, it burned up too. Ain't seen any evidence in here, but we'll have a look around the rest of the building. It's been abandoned since last year. Nobody's supposed to be in here. We did find this, though."

Reilly held out his hand and showed us a wedding ring. I got that thrill of a premonition I get sometimes and picked it up to look at it more closely. Sure enough, there were the initials I'd seen before: VJ and LJ.

I couldn't help but laugh. "Looks as though he got hoist by his own petard, as they say. This is the ring Stefan showed to us at the cemetery. Our problem has taken care of itself. Whatever he was guilty of, he's all washed up now. I can't wait to tell Victoria we can get hitched with a clear conscience."

Flanagan gave me a look. "Maybe you shouldn't oughta act so pleased about it, Jimmy. Might give someone the wrong idea."

"Whataya mean? Why shouldn't I be glad the creep burnt himself up? Good riddance and saves you the trouble of having to get a confession out of him or turn up more evidence. Pretty good outcome all the way around, I'd say."

"Except for Jankowski."

"You're not feeling sorry for him, are you? He likely killed his baby, whether he meant to or not. Wife mysteriously dies. Ran down Daniel and burned up a store that for all he knew, the people living on top of might have burnt too. The guy was a menace. Not to mention playing games with a grieving widow about her late husband. I wouldn't have minded getting my hands on him myself in a dark alley somewhere."

Reilly snorted. "Feeling cheated, Malhaven? You could stomp on his feet. Get it out of your system."

"Don't encourage him," Joey said. "C'mon, Jimmy. You seen

enough for your story. Let's get you out of here before you dig yourself into a hole."

We wandered back outside. I couldn't wipe the grin off my face at the thought the only impediment to the happiest day of my life had been neatly removed. Joey wasn't so thrilled.

"I'd keep your joy to yourself if I was you. Pretty strange he turns up dead. Convenient for you and Victoria."

"You're not implying I had anything to do with it." I laughed, but his expression said he wasn't joking. "Joey, you know me. I might have been tempted to rough the guy up a bit on the way to the station, but I would've turned him in if I'd caught up with him. What's the percentage in offing him?"

"Puts an end to all the questions, don't it? Whether he was Lukasz or not don't matter now. No chance of Victoria accidentally committing bigamy by marrying you. No trial means the name of her husband don't get dragged through the mud, leaving a question mark in people's minds. Best outcome there could be, ain't it?"

"Look, I'm not gonna pretend it ain't a relief to be done with the guy, but you know me better than that, Joey."

"I do, but it ain't up to me. I'll have to make my report and see what the boss thinks."

"What kind of evidence would you even have against me? It's not against the law to shout to the world about what a crook someone is."

"Hopefully, there won't be none other than motive. We'll search the building. Do door-to-doors in the neighborhood. I'm just advising you to keep your amusement over the guy's demise to yourself. You should know as much as anyone how people talk and gossip in this town, and it don't take much to set 'em off. If the connection with Victoria and you and our victim here comes out, people may put two and two together and get five. Watch yourself."

I scoffed a bit, but I could appreciate Joey's concern. I hadn't written about the guy's claims to be Lukasz, but something like that was bound to get out. What's that saying? You tell a secret to one other person, and it's not a secret for very long. I found that out when I got back to the paper to phone Victoria with the news and type up my story only to get yanked into Morty's office.

"What's this dead husband angle?" he barked at me. Morty's no dope. Even though he's the editor, he keeps his ear to the ground and word had obviously gotten round to him.

"The cops told me to sit on it while the manhunt was on."

"Caught him yet?"

"In a manner of speaking."

"Then spill. I wanna big splash for the front page. The whole story this time or you can take a hike, and I'll get somebody else to finish it."

I knew better than to protest. Morty don't waste his breath quarreling with mere reporters. It's his way or the highway. I was faced with a dilemma, but I knew if I didn't write it up, one of the other guys —heck, even Maudie—would relish doing a sensational take. At least I could put my own slant on it to keep the focus off Victoria as much as possible.

But first, I phoned her to let her in on the news and warn her she was gonna be front page fodder again.

"Don't worry, Jim. I've been expecting the story to come out any day. In a way, it's a relief to get it over with. We can put it all behind us and focus on the wedding. I can't help but feel sorry for the man. What a horrible way to die."

"Live by the sword, die by the sword. Seems fitting for a guy who was obsessed with fire. I couldn't help celebrating a bit, but Joey set me straight. I guess you're both right. If we start rejoicing in someone's death, even a no-good like Stefan, it makes us not much better than they are. I just didn't want anything to come between us and our big day."

"Speaking of which, I got the nicest surprise today. Mr. Klein came to visit and brought me the sweetest hat for my wedding outfit. He'd bought enough equipment and supplies to set himself up a corner at Esther's house to work on it. I couldn't believe it with all their other troubles, but he said he was determined to make me one, even if it was the last hat he ever made. Wouldn't let me give him a cent for it."

"Ain't that something. Klein is the real deal. And you done a lot for them. Arranging to get Alice transferred to that Hot Springs place now she's doing better. I'm surprised Klein allowed you to give them the money for that."

"I don't think he would've if it had been for anyone but Alice. He'd do anything for her. They don't know if she'll ever walk again, but the therapies there have shown promise in improving movement."

"It's a wonderful thing to do. But then, you are the most wonderful woman I know."

"And just how many women do you have in your little black book?"

"Never needed one of those. Only one woman for me and I got her number by heart."

"You do say the most romantic things. I'm very lucky."

"I'm the lucky one. Still can't believe my good fortune. Day after tomorrow, you're gonna make me the happiest man that ever lived on the face of this planet. It's gonna be a perfect day."

"A perfect day," Victoria agreed, so at least I wasn't the only one wrong this time.

CHAPTER TWENTY-FIVE

The day of the wedding started out as near perfect as we
could ask for. Sunny skies and warm temperatures, but not
the kind of summer heat that makes you long for cooler fall days. The
wedding was set for 2 pm, and I was looking forward to seeing a crowd
of familiar faces at the courthouse.

Q's mother, Dorothea, was a whiz with needle and thread and had
insisted on whipping me up a new dark gray suit for the occasion. It fit
me like a glove and looked great with my fedora. Wasn't much I could
do about my face. A nice close shave would have to suffice. By way of
Mr. Cressley, Victoria sent me a pink carnation from her own bouquet
to add to the buttonhole on my suit jacket. She wanted me to go ahead
without her so she could surprise me with her outfit, which had been a
closely guarded secret.

After giving Archie a good rub behind the ears for luck, much to
his purring delight, I hopped in the Champ and headed into town. My
mind was racing, and my heart was thumping. I'd never expected to
meet a woman like Victoria, much less be fortunate enough to marry
her. Made me wonder what I'd done to deserve it, but mostly I was just
bursting with the kind of excitement I couldn't remember feeling since
I was a kid when the world still seemed full of possibilities.

I parked and walked to the courthouse steps to find quite a few of our friends already gathered. Mr. and Mrs. Klein had come, and I was taken aback to see Esther and a friendly-looking fellow I assumed was Daniel there too.

"Glad to see you," I said, shaking hands with them all, "but a little surprised. Who's at the hospital?"

"Alice is doing much better. They'll be sending her to Hot Springs by ambulance tomorrow, but we decided we could get away for a short time," Esther replied. "We'll probably skip the reception, but we were at Victoria's first wedding and didn't want to miss the second."

"Lukasz and Victoria were our closest friends once," Daniel agreed. "We should've kept up with her after he died. We worried we reminded her too much of better days."

"Well, you're here now, and I know it will mean a lot to her to see you," I reassured them before moving on to greet Q, his mother, and his sister, Marlene, who was on the arm of Sam Leonard.

"This is looking more and more official," I couldn't help but note.

Sam blushed but Marlene just hung on harder to his arm. "I'd love to make it official. Sam's not sure."

"You know it's not that, Marlene," he protested. "Things aren't so simple in this world."

"They could be if we have some courage."

"Let's not argue. This is a happy occasion."

"Agreed," I said. "And I hope it won't be the last one like it among my friends," I added, though I could understand Sam's pessimism. Marriage between the races wasn't that common and was outlawed in a lot of states. There's no doubt they'd have an uphill battle on their hands if they decided to go down that road. I hoped their love was strong enough to take it.

I was happy to spy Sister Honoria with a contingent of nuns from the Sisters of Mercy. Honoria had been a good friend to Victoria since her days at the orphanage and had agreed to stand up with her. I don't know if that made her a maid or matron of honor. I mean, technically she was married to God, so I guess matron? Either way, I knew Victoria would be happy to have her blessing on the day.

"You're looking quite dapper there, Mr. Malhaven," she said to me in her soft Irish lilt.

"This is about as good as it gets, Sister. Not nearly good enough for someone like Victoria, I know."

"It's what is inside that counts and you have a good heart." She couldn't help but qualify her observation with an "I think."

"I know I'll never let her down. Not if I can help it."

Felt a tug on my suit jacket and looked around to find my old nemesis Mikey Cummings grinning gap-toothed at me. He was accompanied by Mabel and their big sister Margo who I assumed was in charge of keeping an eye on them.

"Hey, Mister, you scared? I'd be scared if I was getting married. It's not too late to get away like Tony Alberts did from Lisa Francini. Ducked out the back of the church and ran off. No one's seen him since. Had a good job at the fire station and everything. Can you imagine giving up being a fireman just to escape from a dame? I would've told her to stuff it. I'm gonna be a fireman when I grow up and drive the firetruck. Turn on the siren and everyone has to get outta your way. They gotta. It's the law. Wouldn't that be something? WA-OO-WA-OO-hey!"

Mikey's imitation of a siren was cut short by Mabel pinching him hard on the arm. Harsh, but that's the only language some understand. Margo rolled her eyes and backed away from her younger siblings as if she didn't want to be associated with the hullabaloo.

"We hope you and Mrs. Jankowski will be very happy," Mabel said. "Don't worry, I'll make sure he doesn't cause a scene."

"You're a good kid," I said, "and you got the patience of a saint."

"She ain't that patient," Mikey said, rubbing his sore arm.

I was gonna argue the point, but it was about time for Victoria to arrive. I didn't want to spoil her grand entrance by having us all milling about outside, so I started ushering everyone in.

I was surprised Joey hadn't turned up yet. I'd asked him to be my best man, returning the favor from his own wedding years before. I figured maybe he was held up on some kinda police business. We'd invited Doreen, of course, but Joey had said she couldn't come, without offering any further explanation, and the look on his face didn't invite any questions. Joey had never let me down before, but I started thinking maybe I could ask Mr. Cressley to stand in if it came down to it.

We filed into the courtroom with the guests taking seats on the hard wooden benches that would be serving as pews. Judge Barlow emerged from his chambers to shake my hand and congratulate me. He was a benevolent-looking old guy who reminded me of my father except he looked as though he actually cared about my big day and sincerely wished me well. Liv and Cressley came in, Liv taking a seat at the front after her glares cleared a space for her.

I beckoned Cressley over and explained my unfortunate lack of best man situation. He kindly agreed to stand with me and take charge of the simple pair of gold bands Victoria and I had picked out. I was afraid for a minute as I was patting down my pockets that I'd left them back at the cottage. It was a relief to find them and hand them over for safekeeping.

The crowd suddenly hushed. I turned to find Sister Honoria walking in a dignified fashion down the aisle to stand opposite me and Cressley. A moment later she was followed by my idea of an angel. Victoria dressed in a filmy pink gown with pearl buttons at the wrists and collar, a pearl necklace she must have got from Liv as I'd never seen it before, and her shining honey hair brushed until it shone, hanging in waves that framed the face I loved most in the world. She sported the cute hat Mr. Klein had made for her with a little net veil that drew attention to her beautiful eyes.

She held a bouquet of pink and white flowers out before her and a smile a mile wide. She held my gaze as she walked, like I was the only person in the world. I can't even begin to describe the feeling it gave me and do it any kind of justice. I only knew I'd never felt as happy in my entire life before. Never even imagined it was possible to feel so good.

Victoria handed over her bouquet to Honoria when she got to my side and took my hand in hers. The judge started saying all the old familiar words. I hadn't been to that many weddings, but I'd seen them in the movies plenty of times and knew when I was supposed to say "I do." I said it so loud and passionately that it caused a few titters in the peanut gallery, but I didn't care who knew how much I meant it.

An exchange of rings and those magic words, "I now pronounce you husband and wife. You may kiss your bride," and we were all hitched up, for better or worse. I knew for me it was all for the better. I was sailing on cloud nine right up until the moment I turned and saw Joey Flanagan headed down the aisle toward me, with Fink and Wilson on either side of him.

Before I could ask what was up, he'd torn my hands away from Victoria's and chucked a pair of cuffs over my wrists.

"James Francis Malhaven, I'm arresting you on a charge of Murder in the First."

CHAPTER TWENTY-SIX

I tried to get Joey to meet my eye as he dragged me toward the door amid the excited clamor of the guests. He did a grand job of ignoring me. Looked back to find Victoria staring at us open-mouthed as Honoria reached over to comfort her. I thought my new wife knew me well enough to understand this was all some kind of mix-up, but there was always part of me believed I didn't deserve her and wondered if there wasn't a part of her that thought the same.

I felt ashamed, like I'd let her down and ruined our wedding. Even if Joey let me go once we got down to the station and I straightened everything out, we couldn't get back that special moment of walking down the aisle arm in arm as a newly-hitched couple being bombarded by well-wishes from our friends and relations.

Joey let Fink and Wilson take over once we were outside. I could've easily thrown them off, but what would be the point? I wasn't gonna take it on the lam for something I didn't do. I let them direct me to the back of the paddy wagon and obligingly climbed in and sat while they joined me and locked the doors. Turns out they weren't great conversationalists, although I tried all my best opening gambits. I resigned myself to waiting until we got to the station to find out what was going on.

They pushed me inside to the desk sergeant who gave me the sympathetic eye while fingerprinting me and confiscating my belongings. I pulled the wedding ring off my finger and handed it over. Hadn't even been there long enough for me to get used to the feel of it. Couldn't help but wince when I heard the clink of metal as it was tossed into an envelope with my keys and loose change. They even took my belt and tie, in case I was of a mind to hang myself out of guilt, I supposed.

I'd taken my hat off back at the courthouse for the ceremony, so I was bareheaded as they bum-rushed me to a cell and slammed the iron bars shut. I sat for a few minutes bemused by my predicament, but then got up and started pacing around like a caged lion with a sore head, scrubbing my hands against my pants to get the rest of the fingerprint ink off. This was not how I had planned to spend the day. I wanted answers, but I'd been around cops long enough to know how they think. They'd leave me to stew for a while in the hopes it would soften me up for a confession.

But a confession of what? Murder? My mind was blank on that until I remembered Joey's attitude when we found Stefan Jankowski burnt to a cinder, or most of him at least. Surely Joey didn't believe I had something to do with it. We might not always see eye to eye, but we'd known each other our whole lives. I found it hard to believe he'd think such a thing of me.

Time had never passed so slow for me in my life before as it did in that cell. On one side of me was a drunk who reeked of booze sleeping it off. On the other, a guy who'd been a little light-fingered with the goods in Mimzy's department store. He was nervous and talkative, but I couldn't tell you what he was jabbering about. I was too busy thinking over my own situation.

Granted, it was a good thing from my point of view that Stefan was dead. There was plenty of evidence he'd been causing havoc ever since he got to town, not the least of which was harassing Victoria and bringing up painful memories for her by pretending to be Lukasz. I couldn't fake any sorrow that he was all washed up, but that was a far cry from being the one to do the deed myself.

I'd almost rather we'd caught him alive. His premature demise was gonna leave way more questions than if we'd had a chance to interrogate him. It would've been better for Victoria to get some answers that wouldn't leave her wondering how he'd come by her husband's things. Even if the truth hurt, she'd never been one to shy away from it. All we had now was a bunch of loose ends and no easy way to tie them up.

Besides, the whole thing was goofy. What did Flanagan think I'd done? Tracked the guy down to that derelict building, asked him politely to take a seat while I lit a match and set him on fire, watching him burn as he made no effort to put out the fire or get away?

Turns out that was exactly what Flanagan thought, more or less anyway. After I'd been cooling my heels the better part of the day, I was rousted out to one of their interrogation rooms with the big two-way mirror. I'd been on the other side of that window often enough, watching the cops grill suspects, to know we'd have an audience.

Flanagan came in and took a seat across the narrow table from me. Fink and Wilson stood behind him smirking. I smirked back. They didn't appreciate that much, but what were they gonna do about it?

"You can wipe that look off your face, Jimmy. This ain't no laughing matter."

"You'll have to excuse me, Joey, if I don't take it too serious, but if you're gonna get tough, maybe I should call a lawyer?"

"Maybe, but let's just have a chat first between two old friends."

"And a half a dozen witnesses?" I asked, pointing toward the mirror.

"It's for your protection as well as ours, you know."

"Thanks. I feel as safe as houses. Best day of my life ruined by my oldest friend."

He had the decency to look ashamed, but he's a stubborn Irishman and didn't give any ground.

"I didn't have no choice. We got evidence tying you to the scene of the crime. No one's above the law, Jimmy. Not even you."

"What evidence could you possibly have? I was never even near the place until I got word of the fire. You escorted me inside yourself. Like I said before, if I'd caught up with the guy, I might have been tempted to give him one in the kisser, but I'd have still turned him over to you. What's the motive for me killing him?"

"Pretty good one if he was Lukasz Jankowski the way he claimed. That would put a crimp in your plans. Victoria might come to believe he was her long-lost hubby after all. Even if she didn't, might not have been so easy to prove he wasn't Lukasz so that she wasn't committing bigamy. Could have drawn out for weeks or months. Ends up in court. Who knows how a judge might rule? Any way it played out, it meant delay and trouble for you and Victoria. I can't say I wouldn't have been tempted myself if I was in your shoes to cut short the wait."

"So, what—I managed to track Stefan down and set him on fire? Wouldn't he have objected to becoming a human torch?"

"Like you suggested, what if you punched him in the kisser first? He wasn't as big a guy as you. Wouldn't have taken much to knock him out and fling a match on him."

"Wouldn't the whole place have burned down? I never heard of that human combustion thing Mike was talking about."

"Me neither, but that makes it all the more plausible because you probably did think the whole joint would burn down and cover up any evidence."

"You keep talking about evidence, but I ain't seen any yet."

Flanagan pulled a paper bag out of his pocket and dumped a cigarette package on the table. It looked as if it had been through the wringer, crumpled, torn and stained, but I could see it was my brand.

"Bennets. So what? I'm not the only ex-GI in town who smokes them. A lot of us got used to them during the war. The Army was handing them out like candy to try to keep morale up."

"It's not so common as you might think. You're the only person who came to my mind when I seen this package."

"You gotta be kidding me. You come hustle me away from my wedding because you found a used package of Bennets at the scene? That's thin even for you chumps," I said, with a glance full of meaning at the dynamic duo of Wilson and Fink.

"It was my call, Jimmy. You had motive and made no secret you were glad he was dead. All I needed was your fingerprints and guess what, they match the ones we found on this pack."

That was a kicker but not for long. "I probably dropped them when I pulled my handkerchief out of my pocket. We was all gagging on the foul smell."

"I'd tend to agree with you, my boy, but we just so happened to find this later when we moved what was left of the body."

"The feet, you mean?"

"Yeah, and guess what one of them was stepping on? This pack with your fingerprint on it. I was with you the whole time we was in the place. Pretty neat trick for you to pick up one of those feet and stick this under it without me or anyone else noticing."

"Yet you're willing to believe I was dumb enough to leave that kind of evidence at the scene of my so-called crime?"

"Maybe as you said, it fell out of your pocket when you was wrestling with the guy and you never noticed. Got anything you want to get off your chest, Jimmy?"

"Like a confession? You can hold your breath for that. C'mon, Joey, this'll never hold up in court."

"That's for the DA to decide. Make it easier on yourself if you own up to it. There'd be plenty of sympathy for offing a guy that was trying to take advantage of a beautiful, grieving widow."

I shook my head, genuinely hurt Joey thought me capable of such a thing. "It's as if you don't know me at all, do you?"

"Maybe I know you too well. Think it over. Take him back to the cells, boys."

Before I could protest, I was marched back down the hallway. The steel door clanged shut behind me with an awfully final ring. I couldn't believe Joey was doing this to me and on such flimsy evidence. I wondered if there wasn't something more to it and itched to be free to investigate. But what could I do? The answer was nothing. I was stuck in a cell for the foreseeable future, and there wasn't one damn thing I could do about it except wonder where Victoria was and what she was thinking.

CHAPTER TWENTY-SEVEN

I stood at the altar, stunned as I watched the police handcuff and escort my new husband down the aisle away from me. We'd only just sealed our union with a kiss. I was dimly aware of Honoria trying to comfort me, but I was focused on Jim's face, looking back at me with pleading in those lovely gray eyes of his.

I knew what he'd be thinking. He didn't believe he was good enough for me or could live up to Lukasz's memory in my mind. He'd never thought much of himself. A holdover from the way his father had treated him. No amount of love from a mother makes it up to a boy who only wants one word of approval or sign of love from an uncaring father.

No matter how much I reassured him that he was the perfect man for me, he always had a sliver of uncertainty. I never had any doubt about him whatsoever though. I could have laughed in Detective Flanagan's face when he announced he was arresting Jim for murder.

Of course, he liked to act tough and could be intimidating when you first met him, with his size and that scar that worries him, though he tries to joke about it like he does about everything he cares about. But I've seen his soft, marshmallowy center, as I loved to tease him.

Murder was the last thing he'd ever do except in self-defense or to protect someone who was in danger.

He had to do a lot of hard things during the war, including killing, but that was the war. We all did things then we would never have thought possible in normal times. He'd come back to the States without any physical wounds, but I knew he still had dreams, nightmares that left him pacing in the dark. And ironically, he'd been wounded worse since he returned home. First the knife attack from a criminal that scarred his face and left him limping in one leg, then the bullet wound in the other that made him feel like an old man when he tried to run or worked too hard in the cemetery.

But oh, when he wrapped those big arms around me in the gentlest hug, I felt safer than I had in years. Cherished and happy beyond anything I'd ever expected again after losing my husband and child. Nothing was going to take that away from me if I could help it.

Mr. Cressley appeared before me with a sympathetic look in his eye and offered me a dark gray fedora. I ran my hands over the soft felt. Jim couldn't have thought any more of that hat if it had been made specially for him. The fact it fit him so perfectly had always seemed like a sign to me that he was to be my second great love after the agony of losing my first.

Our friends crowded around, buzzing with shouted questions and advice. I tried to pull my thoughts together. The next logical step was to go to the police station and find out what was happening. I could only assume they thought Jim had murdered Stefan in order to clear any supposed obstacles to our marriage, but that was just silly. As much as I hated to think about it, Lukasz was dead, his bones resting deep and lonely in the Atlantic. This imposter's claims wouldn't have survived two minutes of scrutiny if we'd had another chance to question him. There were a thousand things I could have asked that only my husband would have known. Intimate things.

Jim would never have denied me the opportunity. Besides, it was his job as a reporter to investigate and uncover the truth. Unanswered questions bothered him. I knew he was disappointed not to have a chance to find out how Stefan had come by the letters and ring. And that poor woman. Nadia. Were we never to know the full story of her heartbreaking past?

I thought back to the strange creature that had flown at me in the cemetery and the story of the *poroniec*. Could it really be the spirit of a baby following its mother to America to help exact revenge? Jim said he didn't believe in such things, but even he couldn't explain away some of the events we'd experienced in the past. Personally, I'd felt Lukasz's spirit hovering close until I no longer needed him, and he could be at peace. I'd also visited Karolina's grave every day since her burial and spoken to her. I wanted her to know she was remembered and loved. What a tragedy for any child to feel otherwise.

A sharp tugging on the soft silk of my dress broke my reverie.

"Hey, lady. What'd they want to go and drag your hubby away for? Did he really off someone? Did he use an axe? That's the best way. Ain't nobody gonna survive being whacked with an axe. I'd use an axe if it was me. Do you think he'll get the chair? Do you think I could watch? That must be something to see. I heard they got smoke coming out of their—"

The rest of Mikey's speculations were cut short by a sharp thwack not with an axe but with his sister Margo's hand. "I am terribly sorry. My brother is so uncouth, and nothing we can do or say seems to make the slightest difference."

With that, the older sister dragged the protesting boy down the aisle while Mabel stopped and shook my unoccupied hand gravely.

"Don't worry," she said, patting the gray hat I still held. "Wrongful arrests are quite common. Charges are often dismissed within a day or two. If not, I'm sure you can have him out on bail soon enough. Let Mr. Malhaven know I'd be happy to assist in any investigation. I am quite intelligent and resourceful."

Despite my anxiousness at Jim's arrest, I couldn't help a small smile as I gravely shook her hand. "You are indeed, Mabel. I know Mr. Malhaven will greatly appreciate the offer."

She nodded, satisfied in that calm, dignified way of hers and followed her siblings' path away from the tumultuous crowd around me.

"I'm going down to the police station," I announced in a loud firm voice to cut through the noise.

"Good idea," said Sister Honoria. "This is outrageous. We'll all go."

"No. I know Detective Flanagan well enough to predict if he feels we're ganging up on him, he'll only dig his heels in harder. It'll be better for me to go alone and have a quiet word with him. Aunt Livinia, could you contact our lawyer's office? I don't know if they take criminal cases, but perhaps they could recommend someone."

She gave me one of her sniffs and a curt nod to let me know in no uncertain terms her feelings about anyone associated with the Wynter family needing a criminal defense lawyer. Given that her father had been a murderous bootlegger and her sisters homicidal drug runners, she didn't really have much moral high ground to stand on, but such inconvenient facts never stopped Livinia.

I extricated myself as gently as I could from my concerned friends, promising to update them all as soon as possible. The precinct house was only a few blocks away. Too impatient to move my car, I strode along the busy sidewalk. Normally, I might have felt embarrassed at the curious looks coming my way. I was rather overdressed for the city streets. But my thoughts were all on Jim and getting him out of whatever trouble he was in. He was my husband now, for better or worse. I regretted we didn't have at least a few hours of better before we got to the worse.

Silence fell among the men gathered in the station lobby as I walked in. They knew why I was there. The desk sergeant was an older man with a kind face. He waved me over.

"Mrs. Jankowski, isn't it?"

"Mrs. Malhaven," I corrected him.

"Ah, yes. I expect I know why you're here then. Come along round the counter and I'll take you to Flanagan's office. I'm thinking he'll be the man you want to see."

"If I can't see my husband."

"Above my pay grade, I'm afraid. You'll have to ask the detective, but don't worry your head none. We treat all our prisoners with the utmost courtesy and respect."

This elicited a barely controlled rumble of snickers from the others standing around, but they had the grace to look shamefaced when I turned to glare at them. I'd learned from Livinia the power of a haughty stare at the right moment.

Flanagan didn't look happy to see me but not surprised either. "Figured you'd be down here before long. I'm sorry about all this, Victoria, but I didn't have much choice. My boss wanted Jimmy picked up ASAP, and I knew where he was going to be so…"

"So, you decided to ruin one of the most important moments of your best friend's life and embarrass him in front of all our guests when you could just as easily have waited until later. You knew we were going to celebrate with a reception at the house. Why on earth couldn't you have postponed by half an hour or so?"

"And only delay the inevitable? Your day was going to be ruined one way or another. I couldn't take a chance on Jimmy making a getaway."

"A getaway?" I had to laugh. "From what? You've known Jim longer than anyone. You must know this charge is absurd. What possible evidence could you have that he murdered someone?"

"The kind that gets men sent to the chair."

CHAPTER TWENTY-EIGHT

It made my knees weak to hear Flanagan speak those words with so much conviction. Perhaps he thought I was going to have the vapors, or some other stereotypically feminine reaction, because he jumped up and ushered me into a chair.

"I'm perfectly fine, but thank you," I said, sitting down. "You sound very sure about it."

"Jimmy wouldn't be cooling his heels in a cell right now if I wasn't."

"What is the evidence?"

"You can't ask me that!"

"I just did." I stared coolly at him as if he was the most fascinatingly grotesque creature I'd ever seen. I'd found most men hated nothing worse than being made to feel even slightly uncomfortable, particularly by a woman.

He squirmed a bit but held his ground. "I'd love to help you and Jimmy out, Victoria. Really I would, but I been on thin ice around here ever since Jimmy let that Ludgate woman get away."

"He didn't let her get away. He was trying to make sure justice would be served. She tortured that poor boy. Starved him to death.

Killed his father and kept his mother and sister prisoner. Not to mention whatever atrocities she participated in during the war."

"All the same, he should have let us handle it. Justice is a job for cops and judges, not vigilantes. I would've charged her."

"I'm sure, but would she have stood trial? It would have come out that our own government was sheltering the Ludgates, known Nazi criminals, enabling their crimes against the Hasselwhite family. I think she would have been quickly removed from your custody and relocated again under a new name."

"We'll never know now, will we? That's the problem with Jimmy. Always striking off on his own. Sticking his nose in and making decisions he's got no right to make. Causes no end of trouble. It was only a matter of time before he landed himself in the soup. He should never have gotten involved in this whole mess once he found out it had a connection to you. That's conflict of interest."

"I thought you were fine with him tagging along while you investigated."

"Only because he kept turning up around every corner until we teamed up. He was always two steps ahead of us, but not so keen to share any tips. Makes you think he might have got a lead on Stefan or Lukasz's whereabouts and struck out on his own again. You gotta admit, it's exactly the kind of thing he would do."

"That man was definitely not my husband, and while Jim may act impulsively sometimes, he would have done nothing more than ask him a few questions before turning him over to you. Jim was as eager as anyone to see justice done for what the Kleins have suffered, not to mention the poor woman at the theater. I suppose we'll never know what happened to her now."

"Seeing as the man who would know was disintegrated except for his feet, no, I don't think he'll be much help to us anymore."

"Jim said the body was badly burned but didn't go into details. Isn't it rather unusual to only have part of the body remaining?"

"It's rare, but I been told it can happen in the right circumstances. Something about fatty deposits in the body burning up and melting like wax in a candle. It's not a nice thing to think about. I'm not surprised

Jim didn't tell you. Not a good way to remember your first husband, if it was your husband."

That reminded me of something I hadn't thought of in a long time. "That's one question we should be able to answer now. I need to see those feet."

The detective rose from his chair, tugging at his collar like it was too tight. "Now, Victoria, it ain't something you want to see. Jimmy'd never let me hear the end of it."

"Jim knows better than to treat me like a child. I insist on seeing them. After all, if the man was Lukasz, it would be my duty as next of kin to identify him."

"But how you gonna identify him from a pair of feet?"

"Easily. I just remembered Lukasz had an accident while he was working at the cemetery. He and the old gardener, Tom Hooper, were lifting a granite monument into place when the chains holding it slipped. It landed on Lukasz's left foot and crushed his toes. The doctor had to amputate the smallest one and the others healed up crookedly. We thought it might disqualify Lukasz from service, but as it didn't interfere with his walking, the Navy medical board allowed it. The injuries were quite distinctive."

He gave me a hard look. "Just remembered, huh? Guess I only got your word for it though. Hooper's dead."

I didn't need the reminder. Tom had been yet another victim of my mother and her twin sister during the final crime spree that led to their own deaths. "There will be medical records at the hospital or in Lukasz's military history if they haven't been destroyed. And Aunt Livinia remembers the accident well, I'm sure. She was greatly annoyed the monument was damaged as she'd have to pay for a replacement. I remember her standing over Lukasz as he was in agony on the ground and berating him for carelessness."

"Sounds like Mrs. Cressley. I'll admit it would be nice to have an answer to one of our questions. This case has been a head scratcher from day one. If you're sure?"

"Positive."

"Do you want to see Jimmy first?"

It was tempting, but it would be a relief to confirm the body wasn't Lukasz and have at least that much good news to report to Jim.

"Feet first, I think."

Flanagan couldn't suppress a chuckle. He escorted me out to his sedan and drove me over to the hospital. We were greeted in the morgue by a dark-skinned man in a white coat. He was as tall as Jim and sported a warm smile.

He held out a hand to me. "I'm Cyrus Timmons, Marquis Sutherland's uncle. He's told me about you and Mr. Malhaven. Thinks a lot of you."

"As we do of him," I replied, pleased to make a friendly connection in such a desolate place.

Detective Flanagan explained what we were there for.

Mr. Timmons shook his head. "They aren't a pretty sight. Not something you're likely to ever forget, ma'am. You sure you want to see them?"

"I appreciate your concern, but they won't be the first unpleasant thing I've had to witness in my life. It's important we clear up any question of my coming so close to being a bigamist."

"Today's your wedding day, isn't it? You look a picture. Where's Mr. Malhaven?"

"Currently incarcerated. Long story," said Flanagan.

"I am truly sorry to hear it," Mr. Timmons replied. "I hope it's not for anything serious."

"Murder," I said, "but it's all a misunderstanding. One I intend to get straightened out, starting with identifying the victim."

"We'd better get to it then. No man wants to spend his wedding night in jail." He walked over to one of the freezer units and pulled out a metal tray. It was draped with a white sheet that was flat except for a bump at the end. Mr. Timmons pulled back the sheet.

It was a gruesome sight, but the feet were more intact than I expected. The ankles and part of the shins were still attached, though badly charred, but the feet themselves were almost untouched by the fire.

"How strange! And the rest of the body was destroyed?"

"Yes. Been in the morgue business a long time, but first I've seen anything like it."

Flanagan and I leaned over for a closer look.

"You see, Detective Flanagan," I pointed out. "All ten toes are there and look normal. Lukasz only had nine and the ones on his left foot were crooked from his accident. These are far hairier than my husband's were too."

"You remember a thing like that?" Flanagan scoffed.

"I remember every inch of my husband's body. Aren't you as familiar with your wife's? I don't think it's so unusual for married couples, is it?" I gave him a meaningful look.

If embarrassment could kill a man, Mr. Timmons would have had another customer to lay out on one of his metal beds right that moment.

CHAPTER TWENTY-NINE

*D*etective Flanagan cleared his throat nervously. "Thanks, Cyrus. We'll have to double check with any medical records we can find, and I'll need to question Mrs. Cressley, but if what Mrs. Malhaven is telling me pans out, we can rule out this Stefan guy being Lukasz Jankowski at least. Has the doc seen 'em?"

"He did an initial examination but wanted to bring in an expert. Apparently, you can tell a lot about a person by their feet. There's a man coming down from Chicago to take a look. I'm sure Dr. Chambers will update you with any additional findings."

"I guess the cause of death is pretty obvious."

"Not necessarily. The body was certainly destroyed by fire, but whether the man was alive at that point is open for debate."

"Well, remind the doc to let me know if they figure anything out that might help us."

"Will do," Mr. Timmons agreed before turning to me. "I certainly hope everything turns out all right for you and Mr. Malhaven. If you need any assistance, I'm sure Marquis would be eager to help. He's a very bright boy."

"He certainly is, and I may well do that. He's helped my husband clear up more than one mystery, so I'd be foolish not to enlist him."

"Now wait a minute," Flanagan objected. "Jimmy's in jail partly because he wouldn't keep out of the investigating business and leave it to the professionals. Don't you make the same mistake, Victoria."

"The biggest mistake I could possibly make would be to sit idly by while you turn my husband into a scapegoat for this situation. I don't suppose it has even occurred to you these remains may not belong to Stefan Jankowski at all?"

"Whataya mean?"

"One of the things we know about this man is he has a history of trying to escape being called to account for any of his actions. You found the wedding ring Stefan showed to me and Jim at the scene of the fire but was there any other evidence as to identity?"

"Well… no."

"How easy would it have been for a known arsonist to set fire to another victim and leave the ring to mislead you into thinking he was dead and thereby stop searching for him? That's a much more sensible explanation than accusing Jim of murder."

"Don't explain the cigarette package though."

"What cigarette package?"

"Forget I said that. No one's supposed to know about it."

"Was it the brand Jim smokes? It's not the most popular, but certainly he can't be the only one in town who uses them. Even Stefan Jankowski might smoke them. Are you saying you arrested Jim on nothing more than a cigarette wrapper anyone might have dropped?"

"A cigarette wrapper with Jimmy's fingerprint on it, if you must know. And we found them under the decedent's foot. Explain that one away if you're so smart."

"Easily. Another plant to throw suspicion onto Jim and reinforce the idea Stefan was the victim. Stefan was out at the cemetery the day he confronted us with his claim. I love Jim dearly, but he isn't the neatest person. I've often found his discarded wrappers myself around the grounds or in his cottage. Stefan could have pocketed one of them with the intention of incriminating Jim."

"I dunno. So far, nothing this guy's done gives me the idea he's planning that far ahead."

"But just think. He somehow obtained my letters and photos and held on to them all these years. If that doesn't speak to someone patient and intelligent enough to be playing a very long game, what does? I wish we knew how he got Lukasz to part with them."

"Stole them maybe?" suggested Mr. Timmons. "I don't know many husbands would give up something so precious willingly."

"I think that more likely," I agreed. "Lukasz was very sentimental about anything to do with me. I can't imagine a scenario in which he would willingly part with them. Especially when he was so far away, and they were his only connection to home. What do you think, Detective Flanagan?"

"To be completely honest, I don't know what to think. We got too many questions and not enough answers."

"All the more reason for you to be glad of any assistance I can give you," I said, turning to leave the room. "I'll be sure and let you know what I find out. Now, please take me to see my husband. Good day, Mr. Timmons."

"Best of luck, ma'am," he called after me.

I strode back down the hallway with Flanagan stomping behind me like an enraged elephant. I could practically feel the heat from his glare burning a hole in my back, but I didn't care. If there was one thing life had taught me, it was not to sit back and wait for other people to solve my problems and having my new husband twiddling his thumbs in jail was definitely a problem. Jim rarely sat still for any length of time. I could only imagine how frustrated he would be cooped up in a cell.

The ride back to the precinct house was silent and tense, broken only by my question of whether I would be allowed to bail Jim out.

"Don't think so," Flanagan replied. "I've never known a judge to set bail in a murder case. The risk of flight is too great. And before you try to explain to me I know Jimmy well enough to know he wouldn't run, it's not up to me, is it? I told my boss about the evidence, and he demanded the arrest. My hands are tied on this one, Victoria, much as I'd like to help Jimmy. And I would. He's my oldest and best friend, no matter what he's done."

I didn't protest. I'd never entirely understood the bond between the two men, other than they had grown up together through rough child-hoods. Perhaps that was enough, although it had become obvious since I'd met Jim that the two often didn't see eye to eye. Maybe Jim's experiences on the battlefield during the war while Flanagan had a safe office job had paved the way for their divergence, or maybe it had always been that way, but Jim was loyal, sometimes to a fault. I knew he'd never abandon the friendship, and I'd never ask him to.

Flanagan escorted me to a room with a table and two chairs and told me to wait. A few minutes later, he ushered Jim in.

"Can't give you more than ten minutes, so make the most of it," he barked before shutting the door. I was surprised but grateful for the privacy.

Jim sat across from me. It was the first time I'd ever seen him at a loss for words, but the look on his face spoke volumes to one who knew it so well. I reached out and took one of his hands in mine and kissed it. He returned the favor, looking relieved. Knowing him, he'd been wondering if I still loved him. He could be a very foolish man.

"Hello, darling. You're not to worry one bit. I'm on the case now," I said.

That got a smile. "I bet Joey's over the moon at the news."

"He did chide me, but you know me well enough to predict how much effect that will have."

Jim stared down at our hands, clasped across the table. "I'm sorry, honey. This is all my fault for not backing out of the whole story when we found out it was personal. I just wanted to protect you, and now I've ruined a day that should've been special."

"It's still special. The day we officially became a team. Us against the world. Admittedly, I didn't think we'd be put to the test quite so soon, but just think what an amusing story this will be to tell our children."

He looked up then, his eyes soft and shining with the kind of love I'd only known once before. "Kiddies, huh? So you made up your mind about that without telling me?"

I don't know why, but that made me blush. "Only if you want them, of course."

"Nothing would make me happier except being with you. But I gotta point out our future don't look too bright right now. I've had a lot of time to think, and I've come to my own decision. I can't have you linked up for life to a murderer. There's only one thing to do. We gotta get an annulment."

And that's when I swatted him. Hard.

CHAPTER THIRTY

"Ow!" he yelled, rubbing the shoulder I'd slapped. "What's the big idea?"

"The big idea is for you to stop being a fool, Jim Malhaven. Don't you dare try to wriggle your way out of this marriage. I caught you fair and square. You can't get away now. You're no more a murderer than I am, and I intend to prove it and get you out of here so we can carry on with our lives."

I filled him in on my visit to the morgue and my theory that Stefan could still be alive and well.

"If the feet aren't Stefan's though, then you still haven't proven Stefan isn't Lukasz," he pointed out. "We could be in even bigger trouble than before now that we've tied the knot on the assumption he was dead either way."

"All the more reason to track Stefan down if he's alive. I'll wrestle him to the ground, pull his shoes and socks off, and take a gander at his tootsies," I teased. "That is if he's managed to find a pair of shoes."

"I'm not sure that guy could find a light in a match factory. We may not know much, but we know he ain't a genius."

"And yet, he may still be at large and about to get away with murder. Murders plural if we count the arson victim and Nadia and perhaps their baby as well. I suggested to Detective Flanagan that Stefan may be alive. I hope the police don't stop looking for him. It would be the perfect time for him to slip away."

"It would be the smart play if the guy has any brains left at all. You know there was a lot of dope in his hotel room when Maudie and I paid a visit. Going off that junk sudden can scramble your noodle unless he's found a new supplier."

"That's a good thought. Might be an investigative avenue to pursue. Perhaps the owner of the feet was a drug dealer? Stefan could have killed him to steal a new supply, then set the fire to muddle the evidence and set the police off on the wrong track."

"Now wait a minute, Victoria. You know I think the world of your ability to handle any situation, but I don't want you wandering around talking to smack pushers. There's a side of this town that ain't safe for decent folks. I should know, I seen plenty of it."

"I wouldn't go alone, of course," I agreed.

Jim shook his head. "I know that look in your eye. If you're set on it, at least take someone who's familiar with the streets like Cressley. He wasn't always a genteel butler and chef, you know. He ran around with your grandfather, old man Wynter, during the bootlegging days. That weren't no walk in the park."

"No, but that was ages ago. Times have changed. Besides, Livinia would have my hide if I involved her husband in anything dangerous."

"As if she wouldn't be furious at her own niece doing the same? Promise me, sweetheart, wife to husband, that you won't put yourself at risk. I'm going crazy in here as it is. What do you think it'll be like wondering what you're up to and me nowhere near to help?"

"Well, I'm going crazy knowing you're locked up for something you didn't do. I know you don't expect me to do nothing. The drug angle is too promising of an idea to pass up, but I will find someone to go with me."

"Like who?"

"Me!" The croak belonged to Maudie Adams, pushing into the room followed closely by a harassed-looking Flanagan.

"I thought I told you to wait outside," he yelled. "No visitors except next of kin."

"Jimmy and me are close enough to be brother and sister. Or mother and son. Or aunt and nephew. Or…"

"I get it, but the point is, you ain't none of those things. What're you doing here anyway?"

"Boss sent me to get the scoop. Jimmy can't exactly do any reporting while he's bunged up in here, can he? Someone's gotta take up the slack. Only caught the tail end, but it sounds like Victoria's got a hot lead."

Flanagan rolled his eyes. "I should lock up the lot of you as menaces to a decent and orderly society. What can I say to convince you to leave off with the police interference?"

"It ain't police nothing! It's just good reporting," Maudie replied. "Is it our fault if we're better at investigating than you bunch of mooks? We ain't breaking any laws."

"That's debatable, but either way, visiting hours are over. Gotta get you back to your cell, Jimmy."

"Can't say he ain't a considerate host," Jim said to me with a thin smile. "You take care of yourself, honey. Only thing could make this mess worse was if something were to happen to you." He sealed the sentiment with a quick kiss before Flanagan hauled him away.

"Don't worry none, Vicky," said Maudie. "Jimmy's a tough nut, but so are you. What's the latest?"

I've always hated being called Vicky, but I knew Maudie meant no harm and it felt good to have an ally, so I let it pass. We sat back down at the table while I went over everything I'd learned since Jim and I had exchanged our wedding vows. The cigarette wrapper, the feet at the morgue, my theory that Stefan was alive, and Jim's idea to pursue where he might be getting his fix if he was still in town.

"Smart thinking. I been around, got contacts. Jimmy's right. You don't quit the hard stuff and keep walking around like nobody's business. I seen guys with the shakes so bad, they couldn't even hold their own pecker to piss, if you'll pardon my French."

I had to laugh. Jim had always told me what a character Maudie was, but I'd never gotten the full effect before. "I appreciate having a partner in crime, so to speak. I'm afraid I don't trust Detective Flanagan to follow up on anything we've learned today, even if Jim is his best friend. I don't think I realized how much trouble he got into when the Ludgate woman disappeared, so I suppose we can't blame him. He has a pension and a wife to think about after all."

"And from what I heard, things ain't so great with the wife neither. Flanagan's an okay cop as far as cops go, but what he lacks is imagination. Jimmy keeps an open mind. That's one of the things that makes him a top-notch reporter. I figure he could get a job at one of the big papers in Chicago if he didn't have a certain reason for sticking around this one-horse town," she added with a wink in my direction.

I felt a twinge of guilt. Jim had never indicated any ambitions beyond his job at the Crier, but I'd hate to think his attachment to me was holding him back. Something for us to discuss seriously when we got the chance. Livinia would protest my moving away, but Chicago wasn't so far that we couldn't visit often.

"Tell you what," Maudie said. "It's getting late in the day and you ain't exactly dressed for snooping. What say we drop in back at the cemetery, fill everyone in on the doings. You can change and get a bite to eat. Can't run forever on your nerves, you know."

I looked down at my wedding gown. I'd been overjoyed earlier when I put it on, but I was starting to hate the sight of it. The day had been a disaster, but I'd had other days as bad. I'd do what I always did, which was pick myself up and keep going.

"Good idea. Mr. Cressley had prepared a wonderful spread for the reception. I wonder if people went there to wait for word?"

"People will go anywhere if there's free food. Take my word for that."

She was right. As we drove up to the Wynter mansion, a crowd came out to greet us, overwhelming me with questions and concern. It was Maudie who ushered me through to the grand stairway inside, promising to fill everyone in while I went upstairs and got changed.

It wasn't until I sat down at my dressing table and stared at the tired face in the mirror that I allowed myself to break down for a moment. I'd always cried my tears in private until Jim came along. I missed his arms around me, his rumbling voice in my ear whispering everything would be okay.

It was only that morning we'd been laughing and teasing each other as we moved his things over from the cottage. I went to the closet and buried my nose in one of his suits to enjoy the scent of him. Turned around and noticed someone had brought Jim's hat along from the wedding ceremony and left it on the bed.

I snatched it up in a panic. Everyone knew putting a hat on a bed was bad luck. We didn't need any more of that. How long would it be before the owner and his favorite piece of apparel were reunited? Not long at all if I had anything to say about it.

CHAPTER THIRTY-ONE

changed into a black suit and low heels more suitable for sleuthing and rejoined the party downstairs. It was naturally a somber affair, but I noticed the spread Mr. Cressley had laid out was well picked over. Honoria brought me a cup of coffee and a plate of finger sandwiches. I'd skipped lunch thinking we'd be back for the reception shortly after the ceremony. Now I realized my stomach was protesting the lack of food. In between nibbles of a roast beef sandwich with a sharp mustard sauce, I answered everyone's questions as best I could, with Maudie jumping in to add her own running commentary.

The elder Kleins had gone to be at the hospital with Alice, but Daniel and Esther had come over to lend their support. Q and his mother and sister. Sam and Mitzi Leonard. Honoria. Even the Cummings had come along. The way Mikey was plowing through the food made his motive plain. Mabel honestly wanted to help, but I got the idea her older sister Margo simply found the whole situation as thrilling as the crime novels she was addicted to. She was soaking it all in to gossip about later with her friends.

Livinia was holding court from the golden velvet armchair that was her seat of choice when the formal parlor was in use. Mr. Cressley was topping up everyone's drinks and generally performing as the perfect host.

"What an absurd situation," Livinia announced to the room at large. "Mr. Malhaven may be many things, but a cold-blooded murderer he is not. I've a good mind to call the mayor and the police commission and get this Flanagan person fired."

"Oh, Aunt Livinia! Please don't do that," I protested. "He's Jim's closest friend, and I know he'd hate for us to cause Detective Flanagan any more trouble. It's not really his fault. They found some evidence at the scene of the crime that they couldn't ignore."

Q came and sat beside me on the sofa. "What kind of evidence?"

"A cigarette wrapper with his fingerprints on it. It was found under the feet of the fire victim."

"Could have been planted. No offence, but I have noticed Mr. Malhaven can be careless with his empty packets."

I smiled. "None taken. I said the very same thing to the detective. I also have a theory the victim may not be Stefan Jankowski at all. Perhaps this fire was just another attempt to cover up his crimes, same as the one at Mr. Klein's."

"How horrible!" Esther cried. "What sort of a maniac is this man? Trying to run down Daniel, burning down the store, pretending he is poor Lukasz, and now this murder. And to think he might still be out there right now. Who knows what he might do next?"

"That's why we're gonna go follow up a lead," said Maudie. "If the cops think they got their man, they ain't gonna waste time looking into theories. We got an idea this hophead can't go long without a fix, so Vicky and me are gonna check out the dope scene in town."

"*Victoria*," Livinia objected, with an almost comical emphasis on my proper name, "will be doing no such thing. The Wynters of Wynter's Hill are not common sleuths, nor do we visit those parts of Carsworth City."

"Says the dame whose own sisters was drug runners," Maudie snorted.

"I cannot deny what is common knowledge, but we all saw where that got them. An eternal resting place beside my father in the family tomb. I've no intention for my niece to follow in their shameful foot-steps. We've had enough scandal in this family to last for many generations."

"Having Jim locked up for murder is hardly going to do our reputation much good, Aunt Livinia," I observed. "Besides, he's my husband and I love him. There's nothing I wouldn't risk to clear his name. And as Esther pointed out, if Stefan is still at large, there's no telling what mischief he'll do next."

"Surely he'll have left town by now," said Daniel. "There is nothing for him here since you are married."

"Unless he thinks he can prove somehow that he is Lukasz and convince a judge to declare him so. Then my marriage to Jim would be null and void, and Stefan could attempt to claim part of my inheritance. The police don't have a lot of hard evidence against him at the moment, even though everything we've seen points to him being guilty of a series of crimes since he came to town."

"And don't forget the poor woman at the movie palace, may she rest in peace," said Honoria. "The circumstances around her death are quite mysterious as well."

"Everything about this story is mysterious," Maudie said. "That's why we gotta get some real, hard evidence and time's a-wasting."

"I disapprove of this most heartily, Victoria," Livinia said, "but at the very least, take a couple of men with you for protection. Mr. Leonard and Mr. Sutherland perhaps."

Maudie clucked her tongue at this suggestion. "We can't go barging into these joints with a whole posse at our backs. Everyone would clam up at the sight. This calls for a woman's soft touch."

"Please don't worry, Aunt Livinia," I added. "We'll be very sensible and cautious, but I'm not going to sit around here and do nothing while Jim's hands are tied. He's taken risks for many of us at one time or another. Now it's our turn."

"That's right, Mrs. Malhaven," Q agreed. "What can the rest of us do to help?"

"I'm not sure. Do you have any ideas?"

"I'm waiting to hear from my contacts in England about whether

Stefan was officially registered there during the war. If we could find out more about him and Nadia and what happened overseas, it might help us understand what is going on now."

"Do we have any idea where Nadia was from? Did it say in the letter they found in her suitcase?" I asked.

"Mr. Malhaven didn't mention it, but maybe the woman they got to translate didn't think it was important?"

"I know Mrs. Gomolka. She's the woman my father recommended," said Esther. "Daniel and I can stop by there and see if she remembers anything else about the letter, unless you think the police would let you look at it?"

"I'd rather not test Detective Flanagan's patience any more than we have to," I said. "I think it's worth your asking her at least."

"Yes," Q agreed. "Let me know if you find out any clues at all to where she is from. I can check and see if there were anything in the papers there. If a house burned down and a baby died, followed by the disappearance of the husband and then his wife, I would think it would have been a big enough story to be reported on."

I nodded in agreement. "Good idea. I assume the police have been working on that aspect in order to notify Nadia's next of kin. If we can't find out any other way, I'll risk asking Detective Flanagan about it, but the less we involve him from this point on, the better. I know Jim wouldn't want us to get his friend in hot water. Better for us to work on our own as much as we can."

"Yeah, Flanagan's got enough on his mind anyway," croaked Maudie. "Trouble on the home front," she added, with a knowing wink aimed around the room in general.

It was the second time she'd made an allusion to trouble between the Flanagans. Although I had met Doreen, I felt remiss I hadn't made more of an effort to get to know her better since Jim and I became a couple. I'd have to remedy that soon, and perhaps get some insight into their problems. It certainly wasn't helping our case to have the detective distracted and frustrated by whatever was going on in his private life.

"What about returning to the scene of the crime at the Royale?

Mitzi has an in with the manager," Sam offered, giving his sister a nudge.

She scowled at him. "Thanks, Sam. I told you that in confidence."

"Ah, c'mon. What's the big deal? You're both adults. She's been going hot and heavy with the manager there."

"Mr. Brighton and I are simply good friends."

"Blake Brighton? The manager?" asked Maudie. "He's the one found the body. Maybe he can give you the inside dope. Let you take a look around. No telling what those goons Fink and Wilson missed. They're the worst."

Mitzi glanced at her wristwatch. "It should be between matinees and the evening showings soon. He might have time to speak with us."

"That would be wonderful," I said. I looked around at the crowd of familiar faces. "If you think of any other lines of inquiry, do let me know. It is so comforting to have friends in times of trouble."

"Don't worry, Vicky," Maudie said. "You and Jim always got our backs. We got yours now."

CHAPTER THIRTY-TWO

I was feeling misty-eyed as our group split up. Not one of them believed Jim was guilty, and I knew they would be willing to do anything if we thought of more avenues to explore. Our problem was having such limited information, and we hadn't the resources or authority of the police at our disposal.

Dorothea Sutherland stopped to speak to me on her way out. "I hope Mr. Malhaven's new suit will survive his stint in the jail. It's one of the finest I've made."

"He's very proud of it. I imagine it's creased a bit, but nothing a little ironing won't straighten out."

"Good, good. And don't forget my brother, Cyrus, might be able to help. You met him, didn't you?"

I nodded. "He did say an expert was coming in to examine what remained of the burn victim. It would be helpful to know what he says."

"I can call Uncle Cyrus and ask him to let us know," Marlene said. "I'm sure he'd be happy to pass on any news informally, as long as you don't let the police know where you got it from."

"Of course. We mustn't do anything that would jeopardize his job or put anyone in danger. That's the last thing Jim would want."

The very last thing he'd want was me going into danger myself, but I knew he respected my independence, unlike a lot of husbands. How fortunate I was to find two such wonderful men in one lifetime. I'd lost the first too soon. I couldn't let it happen again.

Q agreed to head back to the paper and monitor the phone there in case any of us found something useful on our missions that he could do follow-up research on. After enduring one last lecture from Livinia, Maudie and I departed. I wanted to take the Cadillac, but she claimed it would make us too conspicuous. She tried to convince me to climb on the back of her motorbike, but I drew the line at that. We compromised by driving my car back to town and exchanging it for Jim's. The Champ was anything but conspicuous.

Maudie directed me in a rather haphazard manner. She had a tendency to screech "turn left" or "turn right" when we were already halfway through intersections, but we managed to make our way to a part of town I'd never had reason to visit before. I'd grown up as literally a poor orphan, but it didn't take my own experiences to recognize the extreme poverty and misery that surrounded us.

It was early evening, but still light as day being summertime. That didn't discourage a parade of people from peering into the car and losing interest when they saw we weren't likely customers. I felt both very fortunate and very guilty that my life had turned out so differently than theirs. It wouldn't have taken much bad luck for me to have gone down another path entirely.

Meeting Lukasz had changed everything for me. I'd always be grateful to have been shown I was both lovable and worthy of love despite being abandoned as an infant. Even finding out the tortured circumstances of my birth and that I had been wanted by my mother after all had not completely erased the hurt.

Maudie directed me to pull over and park next to a particularly grubby-looking alleyway.

"What's our cover?" she asked.

"Cover?"

"Yeah, we can't just walk in there and start asking questions without having some kind of cover. You know, like you're an addict, or we need some stuff for our poor old mother who's dying of cancer. Some sob story."

"But aren't you known around here? From your reporting, I mean," I hastened to add.

"Right. Good thinking. But I'm not sending you in there alone. Jimmy'd have my hide."

"Why don't we stay close to the truth? We're looking for a man with a scarred face. He's my husband and I'm concerned about him, worried he's gone off the rails because of the pain he's in. You're my friend and agreed to help me search for him."

"I like it. The closer you stick to the truth, the less likely you are to slip up and land us in the soup. You ready?"

"Ready as I'll ever be," I answered, having no idea what to expect.

It certainly wasn't the smart nightclub with tuxedo-clad doormen outside and full orchestra inside serenading guests with the latest hits from the top of the charts. The familiar strains of *In the Cool, Cool, Cool of the Evening* sung by an attractive brunette drifted over to us. An unctuous maître d' escorted us to a table. I don't think he was very impressed by our appearance as he seated us in a dark corner near the back.

"I'd have dressed differently if I'd known we were going to a place like this," I complained to Maudie.

"What were you expecting? A grimy dive? These gents know the highest-paying clientele need to be made comfortable."

"But surely Stefan wouldn't dare venture in here. He was dressed like a hobo and barefoot the last time I saw him."

"He's had plenty of time to get cleaned up since then. Besides, even if he ain't come here, there's not much goes on this side of town that Harry and Floyd don't hear about. An addict with a barbequed face making the rounds looking for smack will've shown up on their radar, but don't take my word for it. Ask 'em yourselves."

Two men were winding their way toward our table, stopping to gladhand and slap the back genially of select customers along the way. They were most ordinary-looking—average height, weight, nondescript features. They gave the strangest impression of being out-of-focus. I could only imagine it was a valuable trait to have in their business, making them harder to identify to any casual witnesses.

There was nothing ordinary about the look in their eyes when they came close to us. Sharp intelligence gleamed, as well as suspicion and menace.

"Floyd Mathers. My brother, Harry. We understand you wished to speak to us, madam?"

I gave them a smile, one of my "dazzlers" as Jim liked to call them. "Indeed. It's very kind of you to take the time. I'm wondering if perhaps you could help me? I'm looking for my husband. He was burned badly in an accident years ago but still suffers terribly from the pain. He's gone missing, and I'm afraid he may be looking for any remedy to relieve his suffering."

"This is a reporter though. I recognize her," Harry said, narrowing his eyes.

I lay a hand on Maudie's arm to forestall any sharp retort she might have blurted out. "That's right, but she's only here today as my friend. Believe me, we have no interest in anything else that's happening here. Only whether you've seen my husband. He might have been poorly dressed, and he has very noticeable burn scars on his face."

"Sounds like the new guy," Floyd said.

"What guy?" asked Harry.

"I told you I hired a new dish washer. He wandered into the kitchen last night, looking for a handout in more ways than one, if you catch my drift. Gave his name as John Doe."

"John Doe? You jerk! I've warned you against hiring junkies. They'll lie and cheat to get their fix and cause nothing but trouble. Now you got civilians down here poking their noses in our business."

"Look, pal," said Maudie. "The lady is telling the truth. We ain't one bit interested in your business. We only wanna locate her hubby. Make sure he's okay, then we'll be out of here. Simple."

"No skin off our nose, I guess," Harry replied sourly.

The brothers escorted us to the noisy, steamy kitchen. We could hardly hear ourselves think over the clatter of dishes and the cooks shouting out orders.

"Where's the new guy?" Floyd called to a man wearing a white chef's hat.

"Said he was stepping outside for a smoke. Think the heat in here was getting to him. He didn't look so good."

Floyd ushered us out a back door into another alleyway. A man was crouched against the side of the building, head down on his crossed arms.

"Stefan!" I called.

He jerked his head up, stared at me, then, you guessed it, ran.

CHAPTER THIRTY-THREE

The low heels I had on were better suited than what I'd worn the last time I chased after Stefan, but I hadn't anticipated how difficult my slim-fitting skirt would make sprinting. I pulled it up as high as I could while maintaining some decency, though in truth, I'd have disrobed if I thought it would help me catch the man who'd caused so much trouble.

By the time we reached the end of the alley, I was gaining on him. I thought he'd try and lose himself in the crowded streets, but he surprised me by turning to face me instead. He was dressed little better than the last time I'd seen him, but he had managed to find a pair of shoes in the interim.

"Hello, sweetheart," he called to me. "I knew you'd find me. It's kind of a relief. Maybe now we can straighten out this whole misunderstanding."

I bit back the harsh denial that was my first impulse when I noticed the Mathers brothers watching us. I decided it was best to keep up the charade.

"Darling!" I strode forward and hooked my arm firmly through his. "You needn't ever run from me. You know I only have your best interests at heart. Come along and we'll sort everything out."

People are always surprised at how strong I am, but I've kept up my gardening work at the cemetery and it builds muscle. I pulled him determinedly along the pavement as a breathless Maudie caught up to us.

"You are still alive, you moocher!" she yelled. "What's the big idea?"

"I don't know what you mean. Why shouldn't I be alive?"

"'Cause there's a pair of feet wearing your name on a toe tag down at the city morgue, that's why."

"I don't know anything about that. I've been keeping a low profile since the police seem to think I had something to do with Nadia's death and the fire at the hat store. I'm a poor man. I don't have the resources to hire a lawyer to clear my name, but you could do it, Victoria. It's what any wife would do for her husband."

"Except you are not my husband. My husband is currently sitting in a jail cell accused of your murder, so we are going straight to the station and show them you're not dead."

"You shouldn't have gone through with the ceremony. That's bigamy. I never thought you would break the law, Daisy!"

If steam could escape your ears the way it does angry characters in cartoons, it would have been pouring from mine at that moment, only we were interrupted by an aerial attack. It was the strange creature from the cemetery swooping down and getting tangled in my hair.

I lost my grip on Stefan's arm and caught just a glimpse of his terrified face before he was on the run again. Maudie and I were too busy batting at whatever was attacking me to pursue him, but as soon as he disappeared from sight, the creature did as well, taking to the skies in a whirlwind of leathery wings and sharp talons.

"What in the heck was that?" Maudie demanded.

I smoothed my hair down in an attempt to regain my composure, both from the unexpected attack and Stefan's determined assurance that I would accept him as Lukasz and help him escape justice.

"I don't know. It, or something similar, attacked me at the cemetery when Jim and I were talking to Stefan on the grounds. I thought it might have something to do with the *poroniec* legend that was spoken of in Nadia's letter, but of course, Jim pooh-poohed the idea."

"He ain't a big fan of the supernatural, is he. I guess he's only open-minded up to a point."

"He just doesn't like questions that don't have logical answers. It's the reporter in him. It is horrible to think about. They're supposed to be the souls of babies who weren't given proper burial. My thoughts keep returning to Nadia losing her child. It's a pain I know only too well. What a sad life for a young woman, and to have it end here, in a strange place, and in all probability at the hands of a man she once loved and trusted."

It wasn't only Jim and I who'd been wronged. This man had left more than one victim in his wake. I couldn't help wondering if Lukasz himself was another. The more I thought about it, the less likely it seemed Stefan could have come into possession of those letters and photos any other way than by stealing them. If he did so with the intent of taking on Lukasz's identity, then it wasn't a great leap to imagine he might have done away with the one person who could without question deny his claim.

In some ways, I supposed it didn't matter. Lukasz was gone either way. But I didn't know which was worse: the thought of him sinking to the bottom of the ocean, cold and alone, or that he might have been betrayed by someone he'd hoped was a long lost relative.

"The good news is, we've proven Stefan is alive and kicking. Flanagan can't hold Jim for his murder now," Maudie said.

"I suppose, though I do wish we could have brought him in with us. It might have solved all of our questions instead of only one. Do you think Flanagan will believe me?"

"It's not just you. I saw him, and everybody in the kitchen can describe him. Aren't too many running around with his looks. We gotta try anyway."

"Agreed."

I drove us to the station only to discover Detective Flanagan had already gone home. None of the other officers were willing to take our statements since he was in charge of the case.

"No problem." Maudie grabbed my arm and guided me back to the street. "I happen to know where he lives. We'll drop in friendly-like and give him the scoop. No need for Jim to spend his wedding night in a cell if he don't have to."

She guided me, with as many confusing directions as before, to the part of town where Jim grew up. Flanagan had inherited his parents' apartment and liked to tease Jim for being too good for the old neighborhood once he moved to the cottage at the cemetery.

The apartment was the left half of the ground floor of a brownstone. Not overly spacious but more than enough room for two. Doreen opened the door and welcomed us in. She was a neat, dark-haired woman with soft brown eyes that mirrored her smile.

"I thought Joey might hear more from you before the end of the day. I know you and Jimmy think the world of each other. Neither of you would ever give up on the other over a misunderstanding, would you?" she asked, sending a pointed stare at her husband, who was sprawled out on the living room sofa with a can of beer and the evening papers spread across his lap.

His grunt seemed to be all the answer she was expecting as she turned back to us. "I'm working on dinner. You're both welcome to stay. We've plenty."

"Yeah," growled Flanagan. "We've no extra mouths to feed, do we?"

"We'd love to join in!" Maudie enthused. "I'm starving. I'll come help you out while Vicky here gives the detective our news."

They exited to the kitchen while Flanagan groaned. "Do I really wanna know what you been doing?"

"I've certainly not been lounging around relaxing while my best friend is locked up in a cell on his wedding day."

"That's not fair. There's nothing I can do about it. The evidence—"

"You don't need to replay that broken record. I've new evidence for you," I said, perching on an armchair across from him. "Stefan Jankowski is alive and well. Maudie and I both saw and talked to him not less than an hour ago, therefore Jim did not murder him."

"If that's true—and that's a big if—then who's the guy Jim did murder?"

"I have no idea who those feet belong to, but obviously not to anyone that Jim had a motive to murder. That is what clinched his arrest, wasn't it? You believed Jim had motive if the victim was Stefan, but there is no reason for him to murder a perfect stranger."

"How do we know it was a stranger? Could be anyone. Someone from Jim's past or present who was threatening his marriage or you. Besides I've only yours and Maudie's word for it that those feet aren't Stefan's. Neither one of you is exactly an unbiased witness."

I'm afraid at that point I quite lost my cool. "Are you being purposely obtuse?"

He stood up, red in the face as I prepared to endure a temper tantrum. The telephone rang. He strode over and snatched it up.

"Yeah, this is Flanagan. Whataya want? What? You sure about it? Okay."

He slammed the receiver down. "Dammit, looks like you're right!"

CHAPTER THIRTY-FOUR

"Who was that?" I asked.

"Doc down at the morgue. They brought in some body part expert. Says the feet belong to a man in his sixties or seventies."

"While we know Stefan is certainly younger than that."

"Yeah, I guess. I mean, do we?"

"Detective Flanagan!"

"Okay, I see your point. And it backs up your tale about seeing Stefan today."

"And makes it more likely it was Stefan trying to frame Jim with that cigarette packet."

"Likely, but not for sure. Is it enough for us to let him go? Not tonight, it ain't. I'm sorry, Victoria. I know none of this is how you and Jimmy expected today to turn out, but I don't have the authority to let him loose without checking with the boss, and he has an ironclad rule not to disturb him after hours unless the entire city is under siege. You might as well go home and get some rest. I promise I'll see what I can do first thing in the morning."

"You may as well do as he says. He's the stubbornest man I know."

Doreen was standing in the kitchen doorway, wiping her hands on her red-checked apron. She looked as if she'd been crying.

Maudie maneuvered around her and took my arm. "We can take a hint, Flanagan, but did anyone every tell you you're a complete and utter dope?"

Before the detective had a chance to get the words he was boiling to say out, Maudie had escorted me through the door.

"I thought we were staying for dinner," I protested. "I know the circumstances might have made for a strained atmosphere, but I wanted to get to know Doreen better."

"Strained atmosphere ain't the half of it, sister. I got the full scoop in the kitchen. You can drop me off at the paper. We'll check in with Q in case anyone else reported in. I'll give you the sad tale on the way."

We loaded ourselves into Jim's car, which started only with much protestation. Almost made me think it realized I was not its true master.

"So, here's the deal," said Maudie. "Doreen's been using birth control ever since she and the hubby got hitched, only he didn't know. Just thought they'd been unlucky with having kiddies, like it wasn't God's plan. But guess who recently found out?"

"Detective Flanagan."

"Yep. Blew his top. Accused her of betrayal. Wanted to know if she was running around behind his back. Things been rocky ever since."

"But why did she keep it from him? Surely that's the kind of things married couples should discuss."

"Not everyone's the same as you and Jimmy, baring their hearts to each other, you know. Doreen was only a kid when they got married. She watched her ma die in childbirth and was terrified of getting pregnant but was too afraid to tell Flanagan. Then later, when they'd been married longer and she weren't so scared and knew him better, she thought he'd never forgive her, and it's looking as though she's right. You gotta feel for her. Not every woman is cut out for motherhood, but every man thinks we are."

"You're right. I'm lucky Jim and I are so open with each other, but

I've met couples who don't have that kind of relationship. What an unhappy situation. Do you think they'll make it up?"

"I dunno. Flanagan is one obstinate bear of a man."

"Not as open-minded as Jim?"

"That's an understatement!"

I slid into a parking space across from the Crier, and we headed down to the newspaper morgue. Q was on the telephone when we appeared at the door, but he nodded his head at us eagerly and waved us in.

"Okay, got it," he said, making notes on a pad of paper before cradling the receiver. "That was Mrs. Nowak."

"Esther? Did they see Mrs. Gomolka?" I asked.

"Yes. There was no address on the letter, but she remembers the paper had a fancy watermark with words in Polish. Unfortunately, she doesn't remember the name of the manufacturer but did recall a few of the words of their motto."

"So, probably purchased in Poland. Also sounds as if it might have been a more expensive paper if it had a noticeable watermark."

"That's what I was thinking. I remember Mr. Malhaven reported that the man known as Stefan Jankowski said he got married because his father-in-law was an important man that he was afraid to cross. Perhaps this woman came from a wealthy background. That makes it even more likely the papers reported something about them. I'm going to call my European research contacts in the morning and see if any of them remember a story like this in the Polish papers or can tell me anything about the paper manufacturer from what we've learned."

"Why not now?" complained Maudie. "Time's a-wasting!"

"It's nearly midnight in some of those places," I reminded her. "We'll have to try and be patient. At least we know now that Stefan is still alive."

"We do?" asked Q.

Maudie filled him in on our adventure in rather more colorful language than I would have used and our subsequent appeal to Detective Flanagan.

Q took careful notes. "This is good news. They'll have to let Mr.

Malhaven go, at least until they identify the body. I mean, the feet that is. Without motive, the evidence of the cigarette packet starts to look pretty meager. What do you think Mr. Jankowski will do next? It's surprising he hasn't left town given that the police are looking for him."

"I got a kind of an idea about that," said Maudie, "but you might not appreciate it, Vicky. What if—and I'm only saying if—he was to bump you off in some way that looks like an accident? What's to stop him from stepping forward, claiming he's your hubby and entitled to your estate?"

"What?" I protested. "That's very far-fetched, surely?"

"I don't know," said Q. "Miss Adams may have a point. This man seems fixated on proving he's Lukasz Jankowski and has gone to rather extraordinary lengths to pursue this aim. I took psychology in college, and we studied cases similar to this. Obsessives can become so focused on their goal that they lose sight of everything else, including logic. The series of failures and shocks he's received since coming to town may only be making him more intent upon his goal rather than less so."

I felt depressed at the idea. "This ill-gotten money I inherited has caused so much trouble. I'd as soon give it away as keep it knowing it was the motive behind all this evil. Livinia would never allow one penny to go to this man if something happens to me."

"She might not have much choice. All he would have to do is convince a judge he really is Lukasz Jankowski. If you were out of the picture to object, the courts might rule in his favor. Whether it's very likely or not is beside the point though. As long as this man has persuaded himself it will work, I could see him pursuing this line of thought. Miss Adams may be right about his plans. You should be very careful, Mrs. Malhaven."

I was torn between laughter and tears at this advice. I knew they had my best interests at heart, but the times I'd met him, Stefan was far more pathetic than frightening. His activities since coming to town had been almost comical in their ineptitude. However, there was nothing funny about that young woman's death, the death of her child, or what had happened to Mr. Klein's shop. Not to mention those feet severed by fire. As foolish as his schemes were, he was causing real tragedy and heartbreak and needed to be stopped.

"What shall we do next?" I asked. "We've probably frightened him away from the Mathers brothers' establishment."

"Did you notice how much he was sweating, though?" said Maudie. "Didn't look so good, did he? I bet he'll be looking for his next fix. I'll go back and talk to the Mathers, ask 'em to keep their ears to the ground. You ain't got any money on you, do you? Bribes go a long way with those types."

I rooted around in my purse for the fifty-dollar bill Livinia insisted I keep on me at all times in case of emergency. I'd always laughed about it, but here was a chance to put it to good use at last. We were about to take leave of Q and split up when we heard pounding footsteps coming down the hallway. Sam and Mitzi Leonard burst through the door in a state of high excitement.

"Look at what we found!" Mitzi crowed.

She handed me a clean popcorn bag.

I peered inside. "A gray pump. Jim said the woman only had one shoe with her when she reached the morgue. Did you find this at the theater?"

"Sure did," said Sam, "and that's not all!"

He pulled a white handkerchief from his suit pocket and carefully unwrapped the object hidden within. A single hypodermic needle.

CHAPTER THIRTY-FIVE

hills ran up my spine at the sight.

"Where'd you find 'em?" asked Maudie.

"Blake—that is, Mr. Brighton," Mitzi said, turning pink, "told us the police didn't do a very thorough search in his opinion. So, the three of us did our own, checking in and around all the seats in the theater. Of course, they've had a lot of showings since then, so we didn't really expect to find anything, but then Blake—that is, Mr. Brighton…"

"Give it up, Mitzie," said her brother. "You're not fooling anyone. Blake had the bright idea to check on the stage and around the curtains. Even got a ladder out so we could check up high around the lights. That's where we found this shoe with the syringe tucked inside it."

"But how did it get way up there?" I asked.

"What if Mr. Jankowski used this needle to inject his wife with something," speculated Q, "then maybe he heard Mr. Brighton coming and panicked. Didn't want to be found with it on him or anywhere near him so he tucked it into one of his wife's shoes and tossed it up into the lighting rig."

Maudie nodded. "Sounds like the kind of damn fool thing that guy would do. Maybe he was gonna go back and retrieve it but hasn't had a chance yet. Too busy with every other fool thing he's been doing."

"If he doesn't know we've found it," said Sam, "maybe there's a chance he'll go back to the theater. We should stake it out. Might be able to catch him in the act."

There were murmurs of agreement and excitement. I hated to be the one to throw cold water on everyone, but I couldn't in good conscience ignore the obvious.

"The first thing we have to do is turn these over to the police. They are very important pieces of evidence in a possible murder case."

This was met with groans, but they knew I was right. Withholding evidence of this magnitude would be just the thing to send Flanagan over the edge. He might even hold on to Jim from sheer frustration and spite, and that was the last thing we wanted.

"We could do both, couldn't we?" asked Q. "Turn this in, but do our own stakeout of the theater?"

"Sure," said Sam. "Why don't you and I head over there tonight? No time to waste with this guy on the loose."

"That's very kind of you," I said. "Why don't you take Jim's car? It will be less conspicuous than the two of you hanging around on foot. You can drive me to my car first, and I'll drop the shoe and syringe by Detective Flanagan's place. I doubt he'll be happy about our finding it when his underlings failed to, but there's nothing else for it. I'll drop you off at home on my way, Mitzi, if you want."

We split up on our separate missions, all promising to touch base in the morning. As I predicted, Flanagan was practically apoplectic when I presented him with our finds, but whether more at our continued interference or the failure of his detectives to discover it first was difficult to discern. I removed myself as quickly as possible having endured quite enough lectures on the dangers of amateur detecting for one day.

I drove home slowly, weary in body and spirit by the unexpected twists and turns the day had taken. My mind dwelled on Jim, twiddling his thumbs in a jail cell. I wondered if he'd be able to get any sleep tonight. I wondered if I would.

The familiar cemetery gates had rarely been such a welcome sight. As I got out of the car to open them and then again to lock them securely behind me, I'll admit I was nervous. I'd long since lost any superstitious fear I might once have had of being in a graveyard at night but knowing Stefan was still at large and having no idea what he might try next was unnerving.

As I parked the car and exited it, Archie running by on the hunt for some small unfortunate creature and the sound of a sudden flap of wings in the dark gave me a fright. Heart racing, I hurriedly let myself in the kitchen door and closed it behind me, leaning against it in exhaustion.

I was relieved to be home and yet, it didn't feel the same as a real homecoming, not without Jim by my side. I twisted the ring on my finger. It wasn't long ago that I finally took off the one Lukasz gave me, and now I wondered if this marriage was to be cursed as well.

In the pitch dark of the kitchen where my mother had ended her own life, I couldn't help but wonder if I was to be followed by tragedy and heartache always. I'd known moments of great joy but too often, they were overshadowed by unspeakable grief. Jim always praised my strength, but how much of it was a façade? Put on so that others wouldn't worry about me, that I wouldn't be a bother.

I'd learned to trust Jim, to be more open with him than anyone since Lukasz, but there were things I hid even from him. Those dark times after I lost husband and child. My burning desire to join them and how close I came to trying more than once. What stayed my hand back then, I'll never know. I'd nothing left to live for, no expectations other than taking care of the cemetery grounds, being of service to the Wynter sisters, though unaware of their soon to be deeper significance in my life.

Meeting Jim changed all that. So much had happened since then, it was difficult to take in. The discovery and loss of a twin sister, the discovery and loss of a mother and an aunt, finding out I was a Wynter too and entitled to a grand inheritance. Our brief fostering of Lily only to find out her mother was alive though her brother was dead. Such a long string of strange and sorrowful occurrences, and through them all, the only constant was Jim.

I thought back to the first time I saw him. I was pulling weeds around my grandfather's tomb, though I had no idea of my relationship to the Wynter patriarch at the time, of course, but I knew the Wynter sisters appreciated my keeping the family mausoleum looking pristine. They were always a remarkably proud family despite their checkered past and present.

A shadow loomed over me. I looked up to see a big man who tipped his hat to me before settling it firmly back on his head. I'd gotten a glimpse of dark auburn hair and flashing gray eyes, but it was the scar that dominated. I was careful not to let it show on my face, but it was shocking at first. More so in imagining what a horrific wound he must have suffered to leave him so cruelly marked.

But it had been a long time since those days. It would be foolish to say I never noticed it, but now when I saw it, it was only another feature of the face I loved dearly. None of us escape this life without scars of one kind or another. Some of us just have the option of hiding them away deep inside. Life had turned Jim cynical, skeptical, but he'd never lost the innate kindness, the goodness that lurked behind his tough exterior. It was the thing I loved most about him.

My reverie was interrupted by the sharp flash of the kitchen light being flicked on.

"Victoria? What are you doing standing about in the dark?" Aunt Livinia was already in her dressing gown, being a big believer in regular and early nights. "I thought I heard your car on the driveway, but you didn't come upstairs."

I sank into one of the chairs around the large table that took up half the kitchen, suddenly too worn out to stand any longer. "I'll be up in a minute, Aunt Livinia. I'm just very, very tired."

"And no wonder. Gallivanting around playing at detecting. I always said no good would come of it when Mr. Malhaven indulged in it, and now I see he has corrupted you as well."

Any other time, I would have argued and defended my husband, but I was too exhausted to go into it again with her. Livinia had come to accept Jim more than I would ever have expected, but there was always a sharp edge to her tongue. None of us escaped her scrutiny or her judgment. She was my aunt and I respected her, but I'd never really love her, not with the complete acceptance and abandon of my love for Lukasz, Karolina, and now Jim.

Livinia seemed taken aback that for once, I did not refute her statement. Let her crow, think she had scored a point. At that moment, I didn't care. All I wanted was to climb the stairs and open our bedroom door to find Jim waiting for me. To have him envelop me in those strong, comforting arms, lay my head against his chest and feel his great heart thrumming beneath my ear. To curl up next to him and feel his eyes on my face, the way he studied me, as if he wanted to memorize every freckle, every wrinkle, and stow it away in his mind as something precious.

Instead, all I found was an empty and dark room, a cold and lonely bed. I picked up Jim's fedora, placed it on my own head in a moment of whimsy, and stared at my reflection in the mirror. Alone again.

I whispered an anguished plea to the night. "Oh, Jim, when will we be together at last as husband and wife?"

CHAPTER THIRTY-SIX

*L*ying in that steel and concrete box, missing Victoria, worrying about her, was one of the longest nights of my life.

I couldn't settle, too restless, wondering what trouble my wife and the rest of my friends were stirring up. Not that I had any right to complain. I'd stirred up plenty of trouble in my time, but now the shoe was on the other foot.

I chortled out loud at the thought. There weren't any shoes on the pair of feet taking it easy down in the morgue. No shoes on Jankowski last time I'd laid eyes on him either. In fact, there seemed to be a conspicuous lack of footwear in this entire situation. Even that poor woman at the theater had lost one. I wondered if the cops ever tracked it down. Another loose end, an unanswered question in a story that was full of them.

If Stefan was alive and Victoria managed to prove it to Flanagan, I thought he'd have to let me loose. The cigarette wrapper'd be the only thing tying me to the crime if the victim wasn't Stefan, and any halfway competent mouthpiece could cast enough doubt on whether it was planted to sway a jury. No, unless they found out who the feet guy was and could connect him to me, I was firmly out of the frame.

Might be wishful thinking was my last thought before finally drifting off to slumberland in the wee hours, but I was pleasantly surprised to find that for once my optimism was rewarded. I was poked awake to see Joey's red face glaring down at me.

"Wakey, wakey, sleepyhead," he sang to me in a sarcastic manner that I forgave, given the early hour and the circumstances. "Time to fly the coop, Red Rooster."

I was touched to hear him deploy my childhood moniker. We used to play at spies with fake code names. I was Red Rooster for my gawky, skinny boyhood self and the auburn hair, natch. He was Pouncing Puma for his alleged stalking and stealth abilities. A lot of water under the bridge since then, not all of it untroubled.

"You letting me loose?" I asked, just to make sure I understood correctly.

"For now. We've confirmed a sighting of Jankowski that Victoria and Maudie had at the Mathers' joint. Plenty of other witnesses saw him too, so we're letting you go for now, but don't even think about leaving town until we get this whole mess straightened out."

"Where would I go? All those near and dear to me are right here." I gave him a friendly punch on the shoulder to drive the point home that I didn't harbor any ill feelings.

"Only doing my job, Jimmy."

"I know. I got no complaints other than I wish you'd come and talked to me first before arresting me at my own wedding, but we'll let bygones be bygones as long as you fill me in on the latest happenings."

"Don't think I wouldn't love to do that very thing, but technically, you're still a suspect. My advice to you is to go home and take it easy. Make up for lost time with Victoria. Let us handle this from here on out. Now, that's my advice. Do I think you'll take it? No. Does that mean I'm gonna rope you into the loop again like before? Not this time."

He sat down beside me where I was perched on the piece of cardboard they called a mattress.

"I gotta be honest with you, Jimmy. My life's a mess right now. I'm hanging on by a thread. Doreen and I are on the outs, and I may be out of a job soon too if I don't catch this Jankowski guy and put a stop to this crazy crime binge he's on. The biggest favor you could do me is to stay out of it."

"Sorry about you and Doreen. Not headed for a bust-up, are you?"

"I dunno. I found out... well, something she'd been hiding from me. Something important. It's a hard thing to know you can't trust the person closest to you in all the world, ain't it?"

"Yeah, that sounds tough, but Doreen's got a heart of gold. Maybe she had a good reason for it. Sometimes, just when you think you can't trust someone you love is when you gotta trust 'em most of all."

He turned to give me the stink eye. "You turning into a philosopher in your old age, Jimmy? Save the sentimental guff for the paying customers. I got a full plate. Get up and out of here before I change my mind."

He didn't have to tell me twice. I made a note to swing by their apartment when I got a chance and see if I could find out from Doreen what was going on between those two lovebirds. I got a way about me makes people tell me secrets. Maybe if I knew what it was all about, I could give Joey some better advice.

The desk sergeant checked me out, handing over the envelope of my worldly possessions. I fished out my ring first thing and set it back in place on my finger. I'd never been a married man before and wanted to make sure the whole world knew about it. Stepped out into a sunny morning, wondering if the Champ was still parked near the courthouse. Decided the fastest and best move was to walk over to the paper and check in with Q. I could call Victoria from there too. Let her know she was no longer hitched to a jailbird.

Smart decision, because when I arrived at the morgue, I found the whole gang was there, or at least enough as made no difference. Q and Marlene, Sam and Maudie, but I only had eyes for one of them, the tall honey-blonde who turned around at the sound of the door opening, her face lighting up like showtime on Broadway when she saw my ugly kisser.

"Jim, darling!"

There was a certain amount of furor caused by my sudden reappearance, but I barely noticed. I was focused on giving back as good as

I got from my lovely wife. When we finally came up for air, the crowd around us gave an appreciative cheer for our enthusiastic reunion.

Unabashed as always, I tipped an imaginary hat to them. "Thanks no doubt to your good work, I find myself a free man, at least for the moment. They still got that cigarette packet with my fingerprint though. I've a good mind to give up smoking."

Victoria laughed. "Oh, Jim, whatever would you do with your hands?"

"I could always fidget with my hat if I had one."

My wife promptly fished my beloved topper from the back of a chair where it had been hanging unnoticed by me. She handed it to me, solemn as a judge.

I settled it in place with a sigh of appreciation. "Now I really feel like a free man. But what's the latest? Anyone care to bring me up to date on what's been happening while I was caged up?"

They all started in to talking at once but yielded the floor to Victoria when she gestured for silence. She was the one who took me through the doings since last we'd talked. My head was whirling with all the new info, and I can't pretend I wasn't a little miffed to find out they hadn't needed me to gather it, but mostly I was relieved to hear Stefan was alive. It meant we still had a chance to get to the bottom of this mystery and put it behind us so Victoria and I could start life together without a threat hanging over us.

"Sounds as if you've got a pretty successful campaign underway, Captain," I congratulated Victoria. "What's next?"

"We were discussing that. Q and Sam need to get some rest. They spent most of the night staking out the theater in your car."

"It's parked outside, Mr. Malhaven. Safe and sound," said Q.

"Not a problem. Glad she could be of use. I take it you didn't see our man?"

"No, but I still think it likely he may try and retrieve the shoe and syringe."

"I agree. We should keep an eye on the joint."

"Don't worry," Victoria said with a light laugh. "Sister Bertha and Sister Martha are currently hidden in a storage room with a good view of the theater stage. I'm sure if you remember them, you'll feel confident in their being able to detain Stefan if they spot him."

I had to chuckle at that myself. Those two nuns weren't no pushovers. I felt kind of sorry for the guy if they were the ones to catch up with him. "So, you got that covered. What else?"

"I'm going to make a few phone calls and send some telegrams before I go home to get some sleep," Q reported. "I want to keep following up on our overseas inquiries as it may take hours or days to hear anything useful back."

"And I'm gonna check out the drug angle some more. That guy looked like he needed a fix bad. He's gotta get it from somewhere," said Maudie.

"I wonder if we should check with the hospital," Marlene suggested. "He may try to steal if he's desperate. I have friends there that I graduated nursing school with. I can try and find out how easy it would be to gain access to the pharmacy."

"That's a good idea too," I approved. "Here I thought I was the bigshot investigative reporter, but it seems you don't need me at all."

"Wrong again, Jim Malhaven," my lovely wife objected. "I need you for something very important."

Being a knucklehead, I said "Oh, yeah? What's that?" before catching a certain look in her eye. Good to know someone still appreciated me.

CHAPTER THIRTY-SEVEN

*V*ictoria and I retreated to the cemetery and spent a pleasant day making up for lost time. Cressley discreetly left food outside our bedroom door around noon, so we didn't have to come downstairs and make small talk with him and Liv while our minds were on other things. He's a treasure and a half, our Mr. Cressley.

We decided it was only right and proper to emerge for dinner and pay our respects, not that we got a lot back. Livinia took the opportunity to regale me with every mistake I'd ever made and every reason why I was not worthy to be Victoria's husband. Since I kinda agreed with her on that point, I just sat and took it. Me and Victoria were still over the moon from being reunited, so most of it sailed past our heads anyways while we gazed dreamily at each other from across the table.

I was helping Cressley clear the dishes when the telephone rang.

"Maybe there's news," Victoria said, jumping up to answer the extension out in the hall.

I followed, lighting a cigarette while listening to the one-sided conversation. I gathered it was Q, and he'd found out something that wasn't nice from Victoria's reaction to it.

She looked troubled as she hung up the telephone.

"Bad news?" I asked.

"Distressing. Q had a return telephone call from one of his contacts. He was right that it was a big story over there. They recognized it from the details he provided. The daughter and infant granddaughter of an important Communist party official in Poland went missing after her husband burned down their house. The husband claimed it was an accident. Nadia escaped the fire, but no trace of the baby was found, and the husband disappeared shortly after."

"Our good friend Stefan Jankowski presumably?"

"Yes. Apparently, Nadia was inconsolable in the days following the fire and began to speak of being followed by her daughter's spirit in the form of this *poroniec*. She became obsessed with tracking Stefan down."

"Explains her turning up here not long after he arrives in town. Wants to find out what happened to the baby."

"That's the most disturbing part. After Nadia left town, the local authorities discovered a hole that had been dug not far from the remains of the house. Inside it was a rattle and… and the impression in the mud of…"

"A baby. A makeshift grave then." I pulled Victoria close. She was shaking, and I wasn't far off it myself.

"What do you think it means, Jim?" she mumbled into my shoulder.

"Nothing pleasant. Seems likely Stefan buried the baby there, before or after setting the fire."

"Alive or dead?"

"Don't bear thinking about, does it."

Victoria shuddered as she pulled back away from me. "What an animal."

"It's pretty obvious he thinks only of himself. I'm beginning to think there's nothing he wouldn't stoop to if he thought it would benefit him. What a trail of misery he's left."

"I had a terrible thought about how he got those letters. Do you think it's possible he… he… killed Lukasz?" A sob escaped her even though I could tell she was trying to keep a stiff upper lip.

"I'm afraid it wouldn't surprise me, honey. Lukasz must have been on the ship manifest if he was reported missing after it was sunk, but no one knows better than me the chaos of war. It's possible he was never even on the ship at all."

"Possible that Stefan killed him and then hid the body somehow?"

"Might not be too hard if they met up in London. That was around the time Germany started shooting those V2 rockets. Caused a lot of damage to the city. Started fires. Easy enough to conceal a body that way or start a fire of his own. We know he ain't shy about lighting a match."

I guided Victoria down onto the small loveseat that sat beside the telephone table. "I hate this. You suffered enough the first time through without having it all drug up again."

"I guess I'd rather know the truth about what happened to Lukasz no matter how unpleasant. There's no point in living with a lie if we have an opportunity to find out where his final resting place really is. What do you think happened to the baby though? The grave was empty."

"Maybe he moved it farther away before he left town. Didn't want it to be found."

"I know you don't want to hear it, Jim, but I can't help thinking about that poor child's spirit wandering the earth. I was talking to Daniel about it. His family is Polish as well, and he's grown up with the legend. The strange creature that attacked me at the cemetery went after me again when Maudie and I were chasing Stefan."

"Why would it attack you though? You're an innocent bystander in all this."

"I don't know except, well, Daniel was telling me a *poroniec* often harasses pregnant women."

My heart leapt into my throat at the implications. "What? Are you trying to tell me something, Victoria?"

"No, that is, I don't think so, though of course it's possible. Would you mind?"

I took her hand in mine. "Of course not. It'd be terrific news, but I think you're putting too much stock into this tale. I didn't get the best look at it, but that thing could've been an overgrown bird of some kind. I heard owls can be pretty aggressive."

She gave me a look of the kind I knew only too well meant I'd said something she thought didn't pass muster. She was usually right. "I know you don't believe a random owl attacked me not once but twice in two entirely different locations."

"Okay, you got me there. These attacks are weird though. I mean, thank goodness it didn't, but it didn't really hurt you in either case, did it? The first time, you tripped and fell, and the second, it just got tangled up in your hair, right? I thought those things had claws."

"That was the other strange thing about it. It's hard to describe, but it felt as though it both did and didn't have weight to it. Almost like, I don't know, a heavy ghost."

"Now you've gone and done it. Said the g-word. You know I got a thing about ghosts."

"I know you don't like to think about it, but whenever we discuss it, you have to admit you don't have a better explanation for many of the things we've experienced. Why is it so hard to believe the evidence of your own eyes?"

"I'm a man of science. Things that don't fit into the natural order don't sit right with me. Maybe it's because I've never been the religious type. You was brought up in the church at the Sisters of Mercy. Daily mass and the blood of the Savior and the Holy Ghost from when you was old enough to toddle. Makes sense it made you more susceptible."

"Be careful, Jim. You're getting dangerously close to calling me a gullible fool."

"I'd never call you or think anything like that about you, sweetheart. You're the smartest, most capable lady I ever met. I think it comes down to you wanting to believe and me not wanting to believe. Even the happiest married couples don't always see eye to eye on everything, do they?"

"I hope not," Victoria said with a smile. "Sounds terribly boring. I'll never mind a good debate with you. Keeps things interesting."

"Relieved to hear it. I'm already on the outs with my best friend. If I thought I was gonna lose my wife, that'd be too much."

"Never. And don't worry about Detective Flanagan. He has a lot on his mind at the moment. He's getting pressure to tie up this case, and there's that trouble with Doreen."

"What kind of trouble?"

"I didn't get a chance to tell you, and I'm not sure it's my story to tell. Maybe you should ask him next time you see him."

"That's an idea," a gruff voice said from the end of the hall. Flanagan in the flesh.

CHAPTER THIRTY-EIGHT

He trod heavily toward us in his big size-ten shoes. "Cressley let me in the kitchen door. Wrote me a note to say you'd gotten an important-sounding phone call."

"What are you doing here?" I enquired politely. "Don't tell me you've come to fit me with handcuffs again."

"No, truth is… maybe we could go outside, Jimmy. No offense, Victoria, but I wanted to ask Jimmy's opinion on a personal matter."

"Of course," she replied. "I'll go help Mr. Cressley finish the washing up."

Joey and I wandered through the double front doors to sit on the cool marble steps. Felt good as it was hot and sticky out even as the sun was going down.

"You said I should ask, so I'm asking. What's up with you and Doreen? I always thought you were as happy as two little lambs frolicking in a spring meadow," I said.

He sighed, wiped a hand across his brow. "I'm kinda shook up, Jimmy. Found out she's been making sure she don't get pregnant this whole time we been together. I ain't made no secret of wanting to have kids, but I just figured it's not meant to be, and all the while, she was making sure it's not. What am I supposed to think about that?"

"Did you ask her why?"

"Didn't have to. I know why. It's obvious she don't wanna have kids. I guess it's the trouble and mess. She's got it pretty good now. Doesn't have to work. Just keeps the house clean and volunteers at the church. A baby would be a disruption, wouldn't it?"

"Sure, but I can't believe you didn't ask her why. That don't sound like the Doreen I know to go behind your back. She must have a pretty important reason for it."

"Honestly, I been too mad to talk to her at all. I even thought about moving out. Thought maybe I could come stay here at your old cottage for a while until I get myself sorted."

"What? I mean, of course you'd be welcome, but that's crazy. You still love her, don't you?"

"I've known she was the only girl for me since I first met her."

"Then don't be a mook. What you gotta do is sit down and have a heart to heart with her without yelling or threatening or being the jackass we both know you can be. Maybe when you hear what she was thinking, there'll be a solution in there that don't involve you splitting up. I may be feeling extra sentimental because I'm a newly married man myself, but you shouldn't oughta break up a good thing over a misunderstanding."

"Some misunderstanding. She's been lying to me for years. Listening to me bare my soul about wanting kids while knowing we wouldn't."

"Must have been tough on her too. She ain't the devious type. Probably broke her up knowing something you didn't, but did you ever stop and ask yourself why she felt she couldn't tell you?"

"Oh, so now it's my fault, is it?" He was practically yelling in my face, fists clenched as if he was thinking about popping me one.

"See? This is what I mean. It's intimidating. You gotta learn to keep your cool. Have a little give and take without blowing your top."

He sighed. "It ain't easy when you feel like you're watching your life go down the drain. If it was only the thing with Doreen, it might not be so bad, but I been getting called onto the carpet in the boss's office every day, sometimes twice a day, because of this damned case.

It couldn't have come at a worse time. I wish this Jankowski jerk had picked any other city on the map to visit. If I let him get away, Jimmy, I'm gonna be all washed up at the department."

"We'll get him, Joey. Don't you worry."

"We?"

"Listen, I feel bad how things went down with the Ludgate woman. I'll admit I wasn't thinking about how it would look for you when she disappeared. Let me help you out now, make it up to you. I know you say you hate it when I get involved, but we've made a good team in the past. I got friends who could be valuable assets. We were just on the phone with Q. He's got contacts overseas. And don't forget, it was Sam and Mitzi who found the shoe and the needle, and Victoria and Maudie who tracked down Stefan."

"While I'm stuck with the dynamic duo of Fink and Wilson, who couldn't detect their way out of a closet even if the light was on and the door was standing wide open. I guess you gotta point. I don't have much to lose, do I?"

"That's the spirit." I thumped him on the back to show my enthusiasm and filled him in on what we'd learned from Q about the baby's grave.

"This Jankowski guy's a real charmer, ain't he?" said Joey. "The doc did tests on the syringe. Found traces of blood on the needle, but the tube was clean."

"No trace of dope? I was thinking Stefan gave the wife an overdose maybe."

"Nope, but get this. You can fill a syringe with air and push it into a blood vessel near the heart. The air bubble causes some kind of bad reaction that makes the heart stop, but it looks like a regular heart attack."

"Really? I thought that was just something in the movies."

"I mean, it takes a lot of air, but this syringe they found was over-sized. Doc took another look at the body and found a needle mark he missed the first time around."

"Big thing to miss," I couldn't help but observe.

"Yeah. Between you and me, Doc Chambers ain't always perfectly sober when he's on the job. Enjoys his three martini lunches. But we got fingerprints off the syringe and the shoe that I'm betting will match up with our bad guy if we can ever get hold of him long enough to ink him. I got a sinking feeling he's long gone by now though. No sign of him today, and no reason for him to keep hanging around knowing we're on the lookout."

"Maudie had a brainstorm about that though. What if he were to knock off Victoria? If he can do it in such a way it looks like an accident and then convince a judge he really is Lukasz, he could make a case for cashing in on some of the Wynter loot."

"That's an awful lot of ifs for him to hang his hat on when he knows he's in the picture for these other crimes. Don't matter how much money you got stashed under your mattress when you're frying in the electric chair."

"You got a point, Joey, but then nothing this guy has done makes him a genius. Q was talking about how mania takes over some people. They stop acting reasonable. I think Stefan's been planning this scam a long time, and he ain't ready to give up on it. Besides, where else does he have to go? As far as we know, he's out of cash, strung out, desperate for a fix. I got a feeling he's still around. I'm planning on sticking close to Victoria until we know for sure. Any guy who'd kill his wife, and maybe his baby too, is up for anything."

"It burns me up to think about that baby lying in a muddy grave. What do you make of it? Sounds like Victoria's bought into this *poroniec* tale."

"Maybe I have," said a sultry voice behind us. "After all, I'm the one who's been attacked twice by something no one can explain."

We got to our feet, probably looking as guilty as two schoolboys caught talking about the teacher.

"No offense meant," Joey said.

"None taken. I know you two prefer to think you're above such things, but I'm willing to believe the evidence of my own eyes. That creature was neither bat nor bird. Perhaps you can explain what it was, Detective Flanagan?"

"I didn't see it. Tell you what, why don't you take me over to where it attacked you? Maybe we can find some kind of evidence. Discarded feather or something."

We walked over near the angel statue and scouted along the ground toward the wall for anything out of place. The sun was going down, but it was still light enough to see.

"What's that?" Victoria said. "I thought I heard something over—"

A black shadow leapt from one of the spreading oak trees that dotted the graveyard and flew close past her head. Joey and I rushed toward her, but by the time we got there, it had disappeared over the wall.

Joey goggled at us. "That ain't no damn bird!"

CHAPTER THIRTY-NINE

Victoria looked smug and rightly so. "Now you see what I'm talking about."

Joey was shook up. "You convinced me it ain't something you see every day, but some kind of demon or ghost? That's a lot to ask. Why does it keep showing up around you?"

"Part of the legend is it's attracted to women who are with child."

"But you and Jim only been married one day. Oh."

Victoria shot me an amused look. I'd forgotten how old-fashioned Joey could be.

"Does that mean…?" he asked.

"Not that I know of, but it isn't out of the question. It might explain why it seems to be following me around."

I objected to that with a bright thought. I do have one from time to time. "But you ain't the only one who was around each time. Stefan was there too. Maybe it's haunting him instead."

"Jim! That means you believe it is a ghost!" Victoria cried.

"Just thinking out loud," I mumbled, feeling like I'd been caught out.

Joey said, "But Stefan isn't here now."

Flanagan and I got the same thought at the same time. I boosted him over the wall, and he called back to us. "Footprints. Whoever it was took off running like a bat from hell was after him, and maybe it was."

"I do believe I'm converting you boys to my side," Victoria crowed.

"I ain't gonna argue that it was a pretty weird-looking thing," Joey conceded from the far side of the wall. "If it was Stefan hanging out over here, we should go after him. He's on foot, he can't have gotten far. I'm gonna follow these prints. Jimmy, why don't you get The Champ and meet me up near the gates. If I ain't caught up with him, we can see if he's on his way back to town."

"Oh, no," said Victoria. "Don't even think about leaving me behind. Me and my husband will meet you."

It was pretty nice being called husband. Gave me a fuzzy, warm feeling inside. Hooking my arm through hers, we hurried back to the Caddy. I pulled a flashlight from the glove compartment and shone it about the grounds as she slowly drove down the drive. We met up with Joey at the gates.

"No luck," he reported, climbing into the backseat. "Let's drive a bit and see if he's on his way back to the city."

We headed toward town a couple of miles, then back the other way past the cemetery in case we were wrong and Stefan was trying to flee the vicinity, but found no joy in either direction.

"Might as well pack it in for tonight," I said. "Unless you want to stake out the movie theater again in case he heads back there."

"I'll put a couple of beat cops on it," Joey said. "Should be Fink and Wilson by rights, but I don't trust those guys. They're the Abbott and Costello of the precinct, only this ain't no joke."

"I can come by the station in the morning. Check in with you."

"Best that you not be seen there, Jimmy. Let's get together at the paper. That'll have to be our unofficial HQ for the moment."

We agreed to meet first thing, and Victoria and I were there bright and early, even though neither of us had gotten as much sleep as might have been prudent.

Marlene Sutherland greeted us. "Q will be here soon. He's picking up some coffee and doughnuts."

"Good idea," I said. "We should've thought of that. What about the rest of the crew?"

"Sam had to work today, and so do I, but I told Sister Honoria I would be in a little late. Mitzi is helping Mr. Klein. He's rented a temporary space and is getting it set up as a workshop and storefront."

"I'm so relieved to hear it," said Victoria. "I was afraid he was feeling too discouraged to start over."

"I think a few days of sitting around with nothing to do changed his mind. He's worked hard all his life. It isn't so easy to give that up."

"My hat's off to him," I said, laying my fedora on the countertop, but I don't think the ladies appreciated my joke. Luckily Q appeared in time to break up any awkward silence and pass around refreshments.

"I have to run soon," said Marlene, picking a powdered doughnut from the box for her breakfast, "but I wanted to wait until you were here to report on what I've found out."

"We're all ears," said I.

"I talked to some of my nursing school friends who got jobs at the hospital. They say the pharmacy supply is kept locked up tight. Security used to be more lax, but with the increase of drug use and overdoses around town, they're more careful now. Only select staff have keys. Anyone who needs access has to get one of them to open up, and they keep strict inventory on what's taken."

"Don't sound like it would be a snap to sneak the dope out then."

"That's what I thought, but then one of them mentioned that one of the pharmacists hadn't been showing up for work. He's an older man, worked there a long time, and is always very reliable. They asked the police to check on him. His apartment was empty, but there was no sign of anything being wrong."

"Older guy, huh? Are you all thinking what I'm thinking?" I asked.

Q nodded. "The pair of feet at the morgue belong to an older gentleman. Perhaps Mr. Jankowski killed him in order to both frame Mr. Malhaven and steal his key to the pharmacy."

"In which case," Victoria chimed in, "he may try to access the drugs there if he hasn't already. Are the hospital staff aware of this?"

Marlene shook her head. "The detective they talked to didn't seem to have put it all together."

"Who was that?"

"He had a funny name. Fink."

I snorted. "Figures."

"What does?" It was Flanagan, sneaking up behind us. He could move soft for a big man when he'd a mind to.

We filled him in on the latest, watching him get even redder in the face than usual. "That bozo again. If he wasn't the boss's son-in-law, he'd have been out on his ear by now. What chance have I got with help like him?"

"That's why you got us," I reassured him. "You and I should head over to the hospital, check out this pharmacy situation."

"And me," Victoria reminded us. "I'm not letting you out of my sight, Husband."

"Good idea, Wife. We need to keep you close in case this Stefan guy has any designs on you."

We split up, Marlene heading to her nursing job at the Sisters of Mercy, and Q manning the fort at the paper in case he got any more phone calls or telegrams that could shed light on Jankowski's past.

The rest of us piled in Victoria's Caddy for the ride over to the hospital. It wasn't far, but we wanted to be ready to give chase or follow up any leads if needed. Joey flashed his badge at the main lobby reception, and we got directed up to the third floor for the pharmacy.

First thing we noticed when we got off the elevator was Fink standing around looking even more pathetic than usual. The second was Stefan Jankowski and the shiny revolver in his hand.

CHAPTER FORTY

"What's the big idea?" yelled Flanagan. Subtle, he ain't.

Stefan swung toward us, waving the gun around and shaking like a leaf in a windstorm, not a good combination when your finger's on a trigger. A shot rang out. Luckily, it went wild, shattering a planter on a nearby table and not doing the fern in it any good.

Screams rang out as staff and visitors ducked and ran. I stepped in front of Victoria but took my fedora off and tossed it onto a nearby chair. Mr. Klein had repaired two bullet holes already. I wasn't taking any chances on a third.

"Careful, there," I said. "I think your aim's a little off."

"Shut up, shut up, shut up!" he yelled, clutching the sides of his head before pointing the gun back in our general direction.

I stuck my hands up to show I meant no harm. "Hey, take it easy. We're here to help. Looks like you ain't feeling too good. Good thing you're in a hospital. They got lots of doctors here that could probably give you something to ease the pain."

"I don't need any help. All of you keep still. Except you, Daisy. Come here."

"That ain't gonna happen," I said, just as I felt Victoria neatly sidestep me and walk forward. I went to grab her back, but Stefan made a threatening gesture with the gun that froze me in my tracks.

Victoria confronted Stefan as if she hadn't a care in the world. No one can tell me my wife ain't got a spine of pure steel.

"What on earth do you expect to do?" she asked. "There's really nowhere for you to go in town where you won't eventually be tracked down. Wouldn't it be better to turn yourself in? The police will make sure you get medical assistance, won't you, Detective Flanagan?"

"Sure," Joey growled so unconvincingly, I wasn't surprised Jankowski didn't buy it.

"I need my pain medication. You!" he called, pointing the gun at Fink and throwing a key at him. "Open the door and get the stuff I asked for before. And no funny business this time or I will shoot the lady."

He grabbed Victoria, pulling her close and holding the gun to her head. It made me go weak at the knees, but she caught my eye, looking so steady that it steadied me.

"Do what he says, Fink!" Joey ordered.

Fink fumbled with the lock on the heavy steel door while Stefan got more and more worked up. To my relief, we finally heard the click as the lock disengaged. Fink took one look around at us, stepped through the door, and slammed it shut behind him, reengaging the lock. We all stared in disbelief at this brazen act of pure cowardice.

Stefan went crazy, keeping his hold on Victoria with one hand while he pounded on the locked door like a madman with the revolver, screaming in what I assumed was Polish, although his voice was so hoarse from his burns it was hard to tell.

Meantime, I guess word had gotten back to the precinct about what was happening. The boys in blue started pouring up out of the stairwell and elevator, guns drawn. I only had eyes for Victoria, my precious Victoria, at the center of a frenzy of lethal metal and emotions running hotter than common sense.

Stepping up and turning my back to Stefan, I positioned myself as a barrier between him and his hostage and the cops. "Let's all take it down an octave or two, ok? I'm sure there's a perfectly reasonable solution to this situation."

And that's when I got shot in the head. To be fair, it was only a graze, but enough to knock me to the ground good. I must've passed out for a minute because I awoke to total pandemonium. Shouts and running footsteps near and far. A kind-looking older woman in a white coat was leaning over me, applying pressure to my head. I sat up, too quick as it turns out since the world turned upside down on me, but I had to know where Victoria was.

"Do be careful, sir. I'm Dr. Loomis. You're a very lucky man. The bullet parted your hair and left a nasty gash, but no permanent damage, I think."

"Good thing I took my hat off," I mumbled, "but why'd I black out?"

"I'm afraid you hit your head against the floor when you fell. You likely have a concussion. Mild hopefully, but we'll need to check you out."

"Ain't got time for that, Doc." I staggered to my feet. "Where's my wife? Is she ok?"

Strong hands caught my arm, helping steady me. It was Joey. "He took off with her, Jimmy. To the roof. There's a stand-off going on. Victoria insisted I come down here and check to see if you were still being counted among the living or not."

"Take me up there."

"You're in no condition. You're bleeding."

"Yeah, you should listen to the boss. You look a wreck." It was Fink, grinning at me as if he hadn't a care in the world.

"Back off, Fink, you complete and utter zero," Joey snarled. "It's not enough you let that guy grab your gun. Oh, no, you had to top it off by almost getting people killed by not following directions and hiding in a closet. If you weren't the captain's son-in-law, I'd give you a fist in the kisser."

"Lucky for me I don't gotta worry about that," I said, giving the goop a satisfying punch in the nose that took me down on top of him, unsteady as I was, but it was totally worth it.

"Oh, dear," Dr. Loomis said, stooping to examine Fink as Joey helped me back up. "I believe you've broken his nose and knocked loose some teeth."

"Good!" Joey and I both said.

The elevator door opened and I climbed in, dragging Joey after me. I mashed the button for the fifth floor which was as high as it went. We had to climb a flight of stairs from there up to the roof. I was seeing double by the time we walked out into the sunshine. It was a beautiful morning with a cool breeze blowing through an ugly scene.

Stefan stood at the edge of the roof along the front side of the hospital. In one hand was the revolver. The other was wrapped like an iron band around Victoria's upper arm.

"Jim! Are you all right?" she called out to me.

"Looks worse than it is, honey," I called, swiping at the blood that wanted to drip down into my eye, as I waded through the sea of cops facing Jankowski with guns drawn. "And my hat's okay too."

She half laughed, half sobbed. "Thank goodness for that."

"Stop right there," Stefan shrieked. His shaking had gotten worse, and his clothes were soaked through with sweat.

I slowed to a halt, feeling none too healthy myself. I braced a hand on one knee, half slumped over to see if the world would stop spinning. "What's the plan, Stefan? You're surrounded. Bet there's this many more cops down below waiting on you."

He glanced nervously over his shoulder and down at the ground before yelling back at me. "It's Lukasz! I'm Lukasz Jankowski! This is my wife, not yours!" he added, pulling so hard at Victoria that she almost lost her balance.

Too close to the edge, too close to the edge kept echoing in my mind as I ran through different scenarios for taking Stefan out without Victoria coming to harm.

Humoring homicidal lunatics hadn't always been the most successful strategy for me, but lacking a better plan, I decided to play along. Try to buy some time.

"Okay, Lukasz. You've convinced me. Sorry about the mix-up. It's not a problem at all. Victoria and I get an annulment, and it's like the whole thing never happened. You two can live happily ever after. The Wynter mansion is a cozy joint and wait until you meet Aunt Liv and Uncle Cornelius. Sweetest, most down-to-earth pair of relatives you could hope to have. There's even a cat named Archie. You fond of cats?"

I wasn't genuinely interested in the guy's taste in pets, which is just as well as I never found out the answer. At that moment, a dark shadow rose up behind Stefan and latched onto him with an unearthly wailing. In a panic, he dropped the gun. Victoria tried to kneel to grab it, but he wouldn't let go of her. She kicked at it with her foot instead and sent it spinning away from him.

I lurched forward with Joey not far behind just as the thing yanked Jankowski off the edge of the roof. Barely had time to lock eyes with Victoria before she was dragged off after.

There was a sickening thud, then silence.

<h1 style="text-align: center">CHAPTER FORTY-ONE</h1>

I went numb from head to toe and couldn't have moved another muscle if my own life depended on it. Joey rushed past me, leaning over the edge.

"Jimmy! She's alive! Come here!" he yelled at me as he reached for something.

That got me going. I ran over and saw Victoria was dangling from some of the fancy decorative molding along the front of the building, clinging on to the rough stone with her fingertips. Flanagan had a hand around one of her wrists while steadying himself with his other. I grabbed her other wrist and between us, we lifted her back up to safety.

She and I both collapsed on the rooftop, holding onto each other. I don't know which of us was crying harder.

"Oh, Mr. Malhaven," she whispered once she caught her breath. "You are a mess."

"So are you, Mrs. Malhaven." I pulled my handkerchief from my suit pocket and dabbed at her cheeks.

"I think you need that more than I do." She took it out of my hands and held it against the oozing wound on my scalp. "What are you trying to do? Break the world record on number of times you can almost get shot through the head without getting shot through the head?"

"Took my hat off this time," I answered smugly. "You see, you can teach an old dog new tricks."

We sat that way a long time, content to touch and be touched when we'd come so close again to being separated forever. It was only last autumn I thought I'd lost her to the grave. Those painful memories rushed in, made fresh by another near miss. I made up my mind right then and there to give up the whole investigative reporter/amateur detective gag. Morty could reassign me to the cute human-interest stories from now on. It wasn't worth putting the woman I loved in danger just to pursue a hot lead and get a crack at the front page.

Joey finally came over to check on us. "That was a close call, Victoria. You okay?"

"My hands are scraped up and my arm's sore from where he was holding it. I suppose he's dead now, and we'll never find out all the answers."

"You'd think so, wouldn't you? But that's where you'd be wrong. Can you believe he survived the plunge?"

"What?" I said. "That's over five stories!"

"He hit the big oak tree in front of the hospital and the awning over the front entrance on his way down. Docs think it broke his momentum. He ain't in great shape. Lot of broken bones and unconscious. They're working on him downstairs in the emergency room, but last I checked, he hadn't passed over to the other side yet."

"I want to talk to him," Victoria said. "I've a right to know the truth of what happened to Lukasz."

"I ain't got a problem with that, but we'll have to wait and see if they can fix him up first. There's not many can survive such a tumble. That guy's got the best and worst luck all at the same time, don't he?"

"He's got something," I griped, "but it's more like a talent for mayhem. I'm beginning to think he's nuttier than my ma's pecan pie."

Victoria rose to her feet. "There is certainly a strange kind of frenzy around his words and actions. Maybe the doctors can evaluate him for insanity if he recovers. He might need specialized treatment."

I toddled to my feet as well, leaning on Flanagan's shoulder to steady myself. "What he needs is locking away in a padded cell and throw away the key. He's a menace to himself and the rest of us."

She took my arm, guiding me back to the stairway and down the stairs. "I don't agree, Jim. If he is mentally unstable, he's not responsible for his actions. Perhaps the right doctor could help. They've made a lot of strides in understanding how to help people like him."

"This might be one of those we'll have to agree to disagree situations. As long as he's far away from us, I don't care what happens to him. You just make sure he don't give you the slip again," I warned Joey.

"Don't worry. We got half the department down there keeping an eye on him. Besides, he's not going anywhere the state he's in."

"That's what you thought last time when Fink and Wilson let him walk out the front door."

"At least I won't have to worry about Fink for a while. The whole department heard about the fiasco today. Even the Captain can't cover for him this time. I expect he'll be on suspension for a while until this all dies down."

"He needs a new line of work. You can tell him the Crier will be looking for an investigative reporter. I'm hanging up my hat, so to speak."

"You don't mean it, Jim," Victoria protested. "You love it."

"Why? Because it keeps putting people I care about in danger? No, thanks. It was fine when I was on my own and had nothing much to lose, but circumstances have changed."

"No need to be hasty," Joey said. "You two have been through a lot. Go home, get some rest. You ain't hardly had a chance to enjoy being hitched. Now Jankowski's under wraps, you should think about getting away, having a real honeymoon."

"That's not a bad idea," I agreed. "Whataya think, honey?"

"Maybe soon, but we're not going anywhere until we see if Stefan wakes up, and I get a chance to talk to him." From the stubborn tilt of her chin, I knew it was pointless to argue. Besides, I was anxious myself to get the full scoop. I might be giving up the reporting game, but I'd never lose my insatiable curiosity. Ma used to tease me about asking so many questions when I was a kid, and it was a habit I'd never lost.

A nurse treated the scrapes on Victoria's hands and bandaged up my head, warning me what to look out for with a concussion. Other than a splitting headache, I wasn't feeling too bad. I certainly wasn't gonna complain. Not with the love of my life by my side, danger past. We were even able to retrieve my hat, waiting patiently on the chair where I'd tossed it. I grimaced as I tried to put it on.

Victoria grabbed it from me. "I think you can go topless just this once," she cracked with a grin.

"You joke, but you know I feel naked without it."

"Better get you home then and out of the public eye!"

"You'll get no argument from me on that score."

Settling into the passenger seat of the Caddy, I closed my eyes as we headed back to the cemetery. For once, I had no urge to stop at the paper and type up a scoop, even though it was a sensational one. Let Maudie have it. She'd done more to stay on top of this story than I had. She deserved the byline.

I did take a moment to phone the morgue when we got home and fill Q in on the latest so he wouldn't be left hanging. He promised to pass the word on to Maudie and the rest of the gang as soon as he could catch up with them.

Victoria and I retreated upstairs before Livinia caught us and interrogated us on our appearance. We got cleaned up a bit and settled onto the bed, just snuggling and enjoying the fact we were both still in the world after the events of the morning.

"You know, we haven't mentioned the thing that grabbed Stefan," Victoria said.

"Yeah, that's gonna make for a thrilling headline in the paper. Morty'll be over the moon."

"You think they'll print it?"

"Sure, too many people up on the roof saw what happened and will want to gab about it. Don't mean we know for sure what it was, but—" I raised one hand as I felt her about to object. "I've no intention of spending the rest of my day arguing about it when there's much better things we could be doing."

"Why, Mr. Malhaven, whatever could you mean?"

"Stomach's rumbling. Let's go downstairs and grab a sandwich."

That earned me a well-deserved pinch in a sensitive area, but I made it up to her by doing whatever she wanted once I was refreshed with a snack. Exhausted by all the day's events, we dozed off in the early evening, not even bothering to answer Mr. Cressley's respectful knock and offer of dinner.

The shrill ring of the telephone extension out on the landing at two in the morning jerked us up. I stumbled into the hall and grabbed the receiver. It was Flanagan with two words.

"He's awake."

CHAPTER FORTY-TWO

e threw on some clothes and raced back to town. There wasn't much traffic that early in the morning, so we made record time. Joey met us out front of the hospital and escorted us to a room on the second floor. The hallway was lined with cops. They weren't taking any chances this go round.

"This is all gonna be off the record," Flanagan said. "We'll be taking a formal statement from him later if he makes it, but I felt as if I owed it to you two to get first shot in case he ain't got long. I'm sticking my neck out."

Victoria lay a hand along his arm. "You're a good friend, Detective. Joseph, if I may call you that."

"Nobody's called me that since my ma died. I'd like it if you did."

"Hate to break up the mutual admiration society," I said, "but my head is killing me. Maybe we can get this over with."

Joey ushered us in. Jankowski looked pitiful, legs and arms encased in plaster casts that were hoisted into the air and held in place with an elaborate metal contraption. I could tell even through the burn scars on his face that his complexion was sallow, sickly and yellow. His eyes were open but dulled. I wouldn't have been surprised to find he'd moved on from our realm except he turned his head to look at us as we entered.

"Daisy," he whispered. "You came."

I felt Victoria tense up next to me, but then she surprised me as she so often does. She stepped forward, pulling a chair alongside the bed but sitting far enough back so Stefan could see her without straining his neck.

"I'm here. How are you feeling?"

"Not so good. Something happened, something bad, but I don't remember."

"That's okay. You're safe now. Do you remember what happened before? Do you remember Nadia? And the baby?"

Tears sprang to his eyes. "I'm so sorry. I don't know what got into me. I had to get away. I wanted to get back to you, but she wouldn't let me go. I did a bad thing, Daisy."

"Did you? What did you do?"

"I set a fire while she was sleeping. The baby was crying. I was afraid she would wake Nadia up while I set the fire, so I buried her in the backyard. I had to make her be quiet. You understand, don't you?"

I don't know how Victoria stayed so calm. Joey and I both started forward, filled with rage, but she gestured us back.

"You made the baby be quiet, but Nadia woke up anyway, didn't she?"

"The house burned up, but Nadia didn't. She wanted to know where the baby was. I told her it burned up with the house, but she wouldn't believe me. Her father and his friends were always watching me, watching me. I thought I'd never get away, but one night, I saw a chance and I ran. I ran to you, Daisy. All the way home to you."

"You did, but why didn't you come to see me right away if you knew I was waiting for you?"

His eyes twitched wildly around the room. "There's a conspiracy against me. Her father has friends everywhere. They were spreading rumors about me. That I was not who I said I was. It wasn't fair. I had to quiet them, quiet the voices."

"So you borrowed a taxi?" she prompted.

"There was a man, pretending to be Daniel. Pretending to be our friend. Do you remember Daniel?"

"I do."

"I tracked him down, passed him in the street. He didn't recognize me. That's when I knew he was an imposter. A dangerous man. A man who would lie. I had to make him be quiet."

"And Nadia?"

He turned his head away. "Why did she come? Why did she come here? There was nothing for her here. I told her there was nothing for her here."

"But she wouldn't listen to you, would she? You needed to make her be quiet. What did you do?"

He turned back to Victoria. "I knew you'd understand. I was a medic, you know. I learned things. It's quite simple and painless. A little air and the heart stops, and then a match to burn down the place so no one would ever know."

"But you didn't burn it down. Why not?"

His eyes grew wide and wilder even than before. "That thing. That thing. You've seen it. It follows me everywhere. It attacked me in my hotel room, and I barely got out alive. Then at the theater, it came out of nowhere and flew at me. I panicked. Got rid of the needle. Ran for the stairs. I don't know what happened after that. Everything was confused."

Victoria leaned over to lay a hand on his shoulder to calm him. "You woke up in the hospital. I was coming to visit you, but you didn't wait for me."

"I'm sorry, Daisy. I didn't know. I would have waited."

"It's all right, but why didn't you speak to me at Mr. Klein's shop?"

"I saw that man." He nodded in my direction. "Recognized the scar on his face. He's a spy. An assassin."

"Is he?"

"Yes, he's been following me. When I saw him at the shop, I knew it was their headquarters. They were collecting information on me and storing it there. I had to burn it down, or they'd never leave me alone."

"I see, but you spoke to this man at the cemetery. Weren't you afraid of him then?"

"Did I?" Stefan furrowed his damaged brow. "I don't remember. I forget things sometimes," he volunteered and had the audacity to smile sweetly at her.

My blood was boiling, but I could appreciate what Victoria was doing. Drawing him out. Whether it was an act on his part or not, at least we were getting some of the dirt on him. He wasn't being shy about confessing to his crimes. Joey and I exchanged a look but kept our gobs shut.

"So, you burned down the hat store?"

"Yes. It was a lovely fire. One of my best. I watched from an alley across the street. It isn't as easy to start a good fire as people think."

"I'm sure. You're very skilled. Why you burned up a man and left nothing but his feet, did you know that? The firemen said they'd never seen anything like it."

"That was very strange, wasn't it? I knocked the old man out and took his shoes and socks. They fit me fine. I got the key too. Then I lit a couple of boxes of matches. I expected the building to burn. I hid outside and watched, but it never did. I went back inside and there were his feet. I stuck an old cigarette wrapper I'd found under them. Clever, aren't I?"

A strange sound burbled out of him. I realized with a chill that he was giggling. It turned into a coughing fit.

Victoria offered him a glass of water, helping to raise his head so he could sip at it.

"Thank you, Daisy. I'm afraid I'm very tired. I need to sleep now." He closed his eyes and turned away.

"Soon, very soon. I've only one more thing to ask, but it's important." She swallowed hard. I knew it hurt her to call him by that name. "Lukasz, can you hear me?"

He opened his eyes and looked at her. "I'm Lukasz," he said emphatically.

"Yes, but I'm wondering if you ever met another man. Someone who claimed to be a Lukasz too? Maybe during the war."

He narrowed his eyes. "That man. Did you know that man? Did you send him to London to find me? He was an imposter too. He wouldn't shut up about you. Going on and on and on. He had no right. He had no right."

Victoria breathed in deeply. "What did you do?"

"I made him be quiet."

CHAPTER FORTY-THREE

I saw a shudder go through Victoria and would have stepped
in then, but again she gestured to us to stay back.

"Did you?" she asked, though her voice was shaking. "Why did
you do that?"

"He stole things from me. Letters. Your photo. He was even
wearing my ring. Sitting there staring at me with that smug face. Said
we were distant cousins. You see, he thought he could pretend to be
me. Isn't it funny, Daisy? Him so handsome, and me like this, and he
thought people would believe him."

"But your face wasn't like this when I first met you."

"It wasn't?" He looked confused again. "But it's always been like
this. Since I was a boy. The barn. That was my first. I'll never forget
the heat, the warmth. It felt so good on my skin. You know this."

"I see. So, a man came to you, said he was your cousin. Said he
was Lukasz, and what did you do?"

"He wouldn't shut up. Why do people talk so much? I only wanted
him to be quiet. I put a cushion over his face. It was red with pink
flowers. I enjoyed looking at it. He was strong, but I was stronger."

I'd never admired Victoria so much as I did at that moment,

watching her listen to this lunatic rave of murdering the man she'd loved as much as she did me. She got so still, I could've sworn she'd turned to stone, but she went on.

"Did you take him somewhere?"

"There were bombs that night. He wanted to go to a shelter when the air sirens sounded, but I couldn't allow it. I needed my things back from him. So I made him be quiet and took my things. I carried him outside. I'm very strong, Daisy."

"Yes."

"It was beautiful outside. I've never seen so many fires in one place before. I put him on one just like a funeral pyre. Did you know the Vikings burn their dead? It's a glorious thing to watch. His uniform caught fire first—Daisy!"

He called after her, but Victoria had had enough. She ran to my arms. I hustled her out of there and away from the evil that poisoned the very air in the room.

Flanagan followed after us. "Sorry you had to hear that."

Victoria was crying softly, silently, tears coursing down her cheeks. "No, it's better this way. I would always have wondered, but now I know," she whispered.

"C'mon, sweetheart, let's get out of here," I said. "There's nothing more to be done, is there, Joey?"

"Not much, thanks to Victoria. A few loose ends to tie up, but I doubt we'd have gotten ten words out of him without your help. It was a smart idea to humor him. The guy obviously lost his whole bag of marbles somewhere along the way."

"Or he's putting on a good act," I added cynically. "Knows he's out of options except pleading insanity."

"Do you think so, Jim?" Victoria asked, pulling a tissue from her purse to dry her eyes, even though it was like trying to stop a waterfall with a hand towel, but who could blame her. It's not every day someone coolly recounts a string of terror to you as if it was no big deal.

"He wouldn't be the first to do it to try and avoid the electric chair.

If he makes it, they'll have to bring in the brain docs to give him a working over. They'll know what to look for. At least he's caught and we know for sure he's not Lukasz, as if there was any doubt."

"Oh!" Victoria suddenly ran back into the hospital room with Flanagan and me left in the hallway staring at each other in surprise.

A high-pitched scream got us moving. We charged through the door to find Victoria cowering in one corner. I caught a glimpse of something big and black, like the shadow of a shadow, before rushing to my wife's side.

"What the hell was that?" Flanagan asked.

"I… I think he's dead," Victoria offered.

Joey went to the head of the bed and felt for Stefan's pulse. "I think you're right." He pushed the emergency call bell, and we waited for the cavalry to ride to the rescue.

A doctor and two nurses rushed in and started fussing around, but we could tell they didn't hold out much hope of resuscitating the guy.

Victoria was trembling in my arms.

"What the heck did you come back in here for?" I asked her.

"Look," she said, pointing at the bed. Jankowski's toes were visible through the ends of his casts. "Ten little piggies." Victoria giggled. "Told you so."

It wasn't that funny. Nothing about the situation was funny, but she couldn't stop laughing.

"That's it," I said. "I'm getting you out of here. You know where to find us, Joey."

"Yeah, good idea. Get some rest. I'll come out tomorrow and fill you in on anything you miss."

I escorted my wife through the lines of cops, who were already gossiping about what was going on, and took her down to the Caddy. Tucked her into the shotgun spot and grabbed the wheel myself. She's not fond of me driving her car normally. Not sure why. I mean, just 'cause I've had a few fender-benders with The Champ is no reason to cast aspersions on my skills.

She didn't complain this time though. Just lay her head back and closed her eyes. Even the strongest of us got limits, and this whole situation had put her through the wringer. It was eerie driving through that pre-dawn time of night. We had the top up but the windows cracked to let in some air. It was sultry and close. A real typical summer night.

I'm not normally a jumpy guy, but I kept glancing in the rearview mirror. The way the shadows played with the moonlight on the road behind us reminded me of that shadow in the hospital room. Not like I thought we were being chased or anything. That would be goofy. I just felt unsettled and on edge.

The massive gray stone walls of the boneyard had never looked so welcome. We pulled up to the gates. Before I could put the car in park, Victoria was out of her side and opening them up. I pulled through and waited for her to close them and hop back in, but she kept standing at the gates as though she was staring at something.

I got out myself and joined her after grabbing the flashlight from the glove compartment. Always be prepared is my motto. "You okay?"

"Look, Jim." She pointed across the road.

There was an old fallen tree there we'd never gotten around to cleaning up. Perched on it was a dark shape. I flicked on the light and shone it over. "What is it?"

"I think it's a raven, but look at the feathers. They're so unusual."

"Yeah, black and white. Maybe it's molting."

The raven squawked like it was insulted.

Victoria shivered.

"It's just a bird. It can't hurt you," I said. "Let's get out of here. We both need some rest."

She stood a moment more. I was wondering whether to try and urge her on, when she turned and got back into the car without a word. I drove us up the long driveway slow. Archie liked to prowl the grounds at night, and he could be hard to see. We didn't need any more tragedy. Not that night. Not ever.

I think both of us were almost too tired to get out of the car, but we made it around to the kitchen door, where we had a better chance of sliding into the house without waking Liv and Cressley. I was fumbling with my key when Victoria grabbed my arm.

This time she didn't say a word. Just pointed.

On one of the tombs closest to the house, a dark shadow waited. Thinking it was Archie, I called his name, but it didn't move. I fished the flashlight out of my suit pocket where I'd stashed it and turned it on.

It was the black and white raven, and it was staring straight at us.

CHAPTER FORTY-FOUR

"Quoth the raven, nevermore." I couldn't help but say it. I'm not the most well-read guy, but even I know that poem.

"What do you think it wants?" Victoria asked.

"Whataya mean? It's only a bird. Why would it want anything?"

"Daniel told me in the legend the *poroniec* sometimes takes the form of a raven. A black and white one."

"Not that again. I thought we agreed if there was such a thing, hypothetically that is, that it was after Stefan. Now that he's dead, what else could it want?"

"We don't know what happened to the child. Stefan said he buried the baby, but we know the grave was empty when it was found."

"Like we thought, he probably moved it farther away from the house when the heat was on before he took a hike. Wanted to do a better job of hiding it. It's too bad Flanagan didn't get a chance to interrogate the guy. You got a lot out of him, but there's always gonna be small details to be cleared up."

"I would hardly call where a murdered child was buried without proper ceremony or blessing a small detail, Jim."

"You know I didn't mean it like that, honey."

She ducked under my arm and snuggled in close. "I know. It

weighs on me though. At least Karolina had a proper funeral and a resting place in consecrated ground. Nadia's baby had nothing. What a waste of a precious life."

You'll have to take my word for it that I was about to say something very profound and comforting, but we was interrupted.

"What on earth is going on down there? Do you have any idea what time it is?" Liv had her hair all up in curlers and did not look pleased with us. I'd forgotten her bedroom was on that side of the house, and she always slept with her windows open.

Victoria called up to her. "I'm sorry, Aunt Livinia. We'll come in and be quiet. Please go back to bed."

"You can rest assured I will, as soon as you stop your shilly-shallying."

With one last glance at the raven, which had begun preening its feathers as though it hadn't a care in the world, we slunk into the house and upstairs, even going so far as to take off our shoes first so we wouldn't give Liv anything else to complain about.

We closed the door to our bedroom with relief. Victoria immediately stretched out on the bed. She was halfway through telling me she would never be able to relax, when she passed out and was soon sleeping like a stone. I was glad for her. She needed a few hours of peace after all she'd been through.

I tried joining her but couldn't settle and ended up pacing in my bare feet back and forth between the two open windows in our room while sucking on a cigarette. My headache was no better, and my brain wouldn't shut up.

What a mess it had all been. Nothing like what we thought starting our married life together would be. I hoped it wasn't an omen, like I hoped that bird wasn't an omen either. We'd both been through tough times before we knew each other. I'd kinda hoped my luck had turned after meeting Victoria. Didn't we deserve a little smooth sailing after the choppy waters we'd had?

But that ain't life, is it? You gotta take the good with the bad. Says it right in the marriage vows, and I'd meant every word of mine. If we stuck together, we could weather any storm. It made me think of Joey and Doreen. I'd always thought them the perfect married couple. Goes to show, you never know what goes on behind closed doors. I hoped they could patch it up. It'd be a shame to throw all those years down the drain without trying at least.

I watched the sky lighten and turn a rosy pink. Caught myself yawning and thought I'd try napping, when I noticed movement out the window. It was that damn bird again, settling onto the point of an obelisk and giving me the evil eye. I'd a good mind to chuck my ashtray at it if I thought my throwing arm was good enough to hit it. Decided the more sensible thing to do would be ignore it and get some shut-eye. Maybe it would get bored and fly away.

Victoria and I must have been pretty exhausted because it was late afternoon before we woke up. My growling stomach jerked me awake. Victoria was lying next to me, gazing upon my ugly mug.

"Got something on my face?" I said, trying to sneak in one of my creaky jokes about my scar.

She didn't dignify it with a response, just reached out a hand and cupped my ragged cheek. I didn't think I'd ever get over her touching the old wound. There'd been a long few months after I was marked when I'd thought I'd never show my face in public again. I'd mostly gotten used to the stares and wisecracks, but nothing had prepared me for the complete love and acceptance Victoria gave me. I didn't know what I'd done to deserve such a woman, but I planned to spend the rest of my life proving she hadn't made a mistake.

"Hello, Husband."

"Hello, Wife."

"Is that your stomach complaining?"

"You know what it's like."

"I do." She smiled. "Shall we venture downstairs?"

"Let's. Maybe we can sneak some food and come back up here without anyone noticing."

We were out of luck there though. As we descended the staircase, we heard voices coming from the grand parlor. Curious, we poked our heads in to find all the usual suspects gathered. I did a quick inventory. Liv was reigning supreme from her favorite armchair, looking somewhat aggrieved at the quality of guest she was entertaining. Sister Honoria, Mitzi, Sam, Q, and Marlene were scattered with plates balanced on their knees. I was more interested in what Maudie was doing, scavenging from quite the spread that Cressley was tending to.

"Mr. Cressley, you are always on top of things, ain't you?" I said, grabbing an empty plate and proceeding to fill it to the brim. "This is the goods right here."

Victoria laughed and poured herself a cup of tea. "Save some for our guests, Jim."

"We've all had plenty," said Sam. "We've been waiting for you."

"They've been waiting quite some time," Liv added. She wanted to make sure we didn't miss out on the tremendous personal sacrifice she had made by playing hostess or the fact she thought we'd been malingering.

Mitzi made room for us both on the sofa where she was sitting. "How are you doing?"

"Better for the rest," Victoria said. "But it is a lot to process."

"Miss Adams and Q filled us in on some of what happened," said Marlene. "How is your head, Mr. Malhaven? Concussions can be very serious."

"Not too bad, Nurse. A little sore but could have been worse, for all of us," I added, flashing back to Victoria's near miss.

Sister Honoria chimed in. "An angel must have been looking out for you both. Such close calls."

"I can't believe I missed out on it all," Maudie complained. "There's nothing like an eyewitness account to give a story the gas."

"It must feel good to finally get a front-page byline," I said.

There was a heavy silence. Maudie looked as though I'd stabbed her in the gut.

Q spoke softly. "Mr. Quigsby assigned another reporter to the story when he heard you wouldn't be writing it."

"What for, Maudie? You're the one who's been working the beat."

"Front page is for the boys, Jimmy. You should know that by now."

"That ain't right. I'll talk to him. Even go over his head to Carsworth if I gotta. You've more experience than the rest of us put together. I bet you could even figure out all those loose ends, like the train station locker key. Did the police ever track it down?"

Flanagan appeared in the doorway as if on cue. "We did. Just today."

Victoria turned toward him. "What was in it?"

He looked uncomfortable. "I don't care to say in mixed company."

Liv didn't appreciate that. As much as she pretended not to be interested, she was as curious as the rest of us and didn't want to be left out. "Don't be absurd. We're all adults here. What was in the locker? Spit it out, man."

He kept his eye on Victoria, and I somehow knew we wouldn't like the answer.

"The baby. Celestyna."

CHAPTER FORTY-FIVE

lanagan's bombshell was met with gasps. Those of us still eating put down our plates, appetites gone.

Victoria was first to speak. "Whatever can you mean? The baby was in the train locker?"

"Like I said, it's not something to speak of in nice company, but if you're all determined to hear it, I'll give it to you."

No one spoke up, but no one left the room either.

Joey sighed. "Okay. I assigned a guy to catch the same train Nadia took and ride it from Chicago to New York, checking all the lockers at the stations along the way. He was almost to the Big Apple when he found it. He knew as soon as he asked the station master. They'd been having complaints about a bad smell at the locker number that matched the key. Pulled out a suitcase looked as though it came from the same set as the one Nadia had. I won't say more. What was inside wasn't pretty."

"How horrible," Honoria said, crossing herself and sending a whispered prayer up to heaven. I hoped if there was anyone up there that they caught it. Sometimes it was hard to believe how cruel the world could be.

"Do you think the Jankowski guy brought it all the way to America? Sounds like the kind of dopey thing he'd do," said Maudie, "then dump it when it started to smell."

Victoria gave out with a little moan, and Mitzi reached over to grab her hand to comfort her. I grabbed the other one and gave it a squeeze.

"We think it was Nadia who brought it with her. It was her suitcase set, and we found the key in her purse. I'm thinking she found the baby's grave and dug it up with some idea of confronting Stefan with the evidence. She was hellbent on having her revenge on him. But after the boat trip to America and a day on the train, well…" Joey trailed off, but we could fill in the blanks. The stench got too bad, and she was afraid she'd attract attention.

"How extremely distasteful," Liv sniffed, handing out a candidate for understatement of the year award.

Sam Leonard was more forceful. "Good thing that guy's already dead, or I'd be tempted to give him a beating he'd never forget."

"You ain't the only one," I said, "but I guess that fall was too much for him."

"It wasn't his injuries that killed him though." Joey dropped that little tidbit and stood back waiting for a reaction. He got plenty, as everyone started asking the same question at once.

He held up a hand for quiet. "We got the doc to rush the autopsy. He died of suffocation. Deliberate. He was murdered. What happened in that room before Jim and I came in, Victoria?"

I stood up at that, ready to throw my own punches. "I know you ain't accusing her of having anything to do with it."

"Don't be silly, Jim." Victoria tugged on my arm and dragged me back down on the sofa. "I wasn't in there alone long enough to kill a man."

Joey nodded. "Yeah, Jimmy, take it easy. Just trying to clear up a few things."

"You can't blame me for being jumpy, old pal. You're the one who tried to pin a murder on me."

"Like boys in the schoolyard, the two of you," Maudie complained. "Shut up and let Vicky talk."

"Thank you, Maudie," Victoria replied. "To answer your question,

Detective, when I walked into the room, Stefan's face was covered with a dark shadow. He was struggling, but then he went still. I screamed, and the two of you came running. And I know you saw it too, so don't try and tell me I was imagining things."

Joey grimaced. "I don't know what I saw, but the fact is there was bruising around his face and mouth that are consistent with being smothered."

"It's so eerie," said Victoria. "It's just like what he did to Lukasz."

"Poetic justice if you ask me," said I. "Ain't nobody gonna be crying over his grave. We know he was a murderer four times over at least, and that's the ones we know about. He could have used the trick with the syringe before and no one the wiser. I wonder where he picked it up?"

Q answered. "I may have something to add on that point. One of my contacts was successful in tracing Mr. Jankowski from the wartime registration records. He was listed as being an orderly at a hospital in London."

"Makes sense," said Joey. "Probably disqualified from military service because of his burns."

"Yes. He must have returned to Poland after the war, and that's where he met his wife."

"Poor woman," said Honoria. "That was a very unlucky day for her indeed."

"Guess that clears most everything up except whether the guy was actually loony or just stupid," said Maudie.

Joey cleared his throat. "I got some news on that too, only it really ain't fit for ladies' ears."

That earned him a round of disgusted sniffs from the female contingent.

"Well, you asked for it. Don't say I didn't warn you. Doc Chambers found out the guy was suffering from syphilis and had been for a long time. If left untreated, it affects the brain. Turns you nuttier than a fruitcake."

Marlene nodded. "It's a terrible disease. That would explain his irrational behavior."

"Don't excuse it though," Joey said. "If he'd lived, I'd have fought for the chair all the same."

"What a deplorably sordid tale," Liv decried, rising from her seat with all the impatient majesty of an aristocrat tired of mingling with the peasants. "I hope we need hear no more about it." She swept from the room, and that started a general breakup of the party.

Victoria pulled Joey aside. "What will become of Celestyna and her mother?"

"We sent a telegram to the family in Poland. They'd rather they were given proper burial here rather than shipped back overseas again. Said they want them to be at rest as soon as possible."

"Could the baby's remains be sent here to be reunited with her mother?"

"Sure, I guess. They took 'em to an undertaker and got a lead-lined coffin. They're just waiting to hear from us what to do about it."

"I want to bury Celestyna here at the cemetery, Joseph," Victoria said, "along with Nadia."

"You sure, honey?" I asked. "Won't it bring back bad memories every time you see the graves?"

"I feel a kinship with Nadia that's hard to explain. We both lost our babies and were both wronged by the same man. She deserves more than to end up separated from her child in some anonymous grave where no one remembers her story or cares. I will see them united in death, so no trying to talk me out of it."

And I didn't, because I agreed with her. I guess their spirits were long gone, but it was still satisfying to help put the headstone in place over the grave. We buried them together in the plot next to Victoria's daughter. Now she has three souls she visits every day, and there is a fourth that is never far from her thoughts either, though his remains will never be found.

I couldn't help but feel guilty sometimes about Lukasz. He'd gotten the raw end of the deal, while I ended up with the best woman in the world. But then I thought about how special it was to be remembered with such fierce devotion by those among the living. I hoped when my time came, I could say as much.

We took a seat on the bench in front of the cottage on the day we set the grave marker for Nadia and her daughter. Victoria hadn't gotten around to hiring a new caretaker yet, so the cottage was sitting empty. We still enjoyed watching the sunset from there, her tucked up under my arm, us talking in low voices about the events of the day and our hopes for the future.

Archie was lazing at our feet when he suddenly came to life, hissing and spitting. The black and white raven was back, sitting on a cracked tombstone. You don't have to believe me, but I'd swear it nodded at us before taking flight in a silent flutter of wings into the setting sun. We never saw it again. Victoria said it meant Celestyna was now at peace.

I hoped so. Babies deserve nothing but love and protection in this world. I knew that's what mine and Victoria's was gonna get. Now if we could only agree on a name.

ABOUT THE AUTHOR

Helen Whistberry is an indie author and artist who took up writing after retiring from a long career working in libraries. She has published three books in her Jim Malhaven Mysteries series, light noir novels with a cozy mystery feel and a touch of the paranormal that pay loving tribute to the wise guy detectives of the 1940s and '50s; and a Christmas-themed Gothic ghost tale as well as contributing short stories to numerous anthologies. When not writing or drawing, she enjoys exploring the natural world of the Southeastern United States and loves all animals, including her two cats and a rather silly six-pound Chihuahua. She also loves to read and review books by fellow indie authors. You can find out more about her books, art, and book reviews by visiting

www.helenwhistberry.com

Thank you so much for reading *The Ghostly Groom*. I hope you enjoyed reading it as much as I enjoyed writing it!

www.ingramcontent.com/pod-product-compliance
Lightning Source LLC
Chambersburg PA
CBHW061619190726
48288CB00007B/2389